PENGUIN CLASSICS

PINOCCHIO

CARLO COLLODI (1826–1890) was the pen name of Carlo Loren-zini, an Italian journalist born in Florence. Collodi's life and writings were dedicated to the struggles of the *Risorgimento*—the Italian liberation movement to free the country from Aus-trian domination and establish a national identity. As a soldier, Collodi took part in several revolutionary campaigns. He also founded *Il Lampione*, a newspaper of political satire whose cir-culation was frequently blocked by the Austrians. In 1875, Col-lodi put aside his political struggles and turned to a new interest. He wrote to a friend: "Now I shall devote myself to writing only for children. Grown-ups are too hard to satisfy; they are not for me." In 1881, the first chapter of *Pinocchio* appeared in the *Giornale dei Bambini*, and it was an immediate success. The complete *Pinocchio* first appeared in book form in 1883.

JACK ZIPES is a professor of German at the University of Min-nesota. A specialist in folklore, fairy tales, and children's litera-ture, he has translated such works as the fairy tales of the Brothers Grimm and Hermann Hesse, written several books of criticism, and edited numerous anthologies including *Spells of Enchantment: The Wondrous Fairy Tales of Western Culture* (Penguin). He also edited *The Wonderful World of Oz*, an om-nibus comprising L. Frank Baum's *The Wizard of Oz*, *The Emerald City of Oz*, and *Glinda of Oz*, for Penguin Classics. He has been honored with the Distinguished Scholar Award by the International Association for the Fantastic in the Arts.

CARLO COLLODI

Pinocchio

THE TALE OF A PUPPET

The Original Translation by
M. A. MURRAY

•

Revised by
G. TASSINARI

•

Illustrated by
CHARLES FOLKARD

•

Introduction by
JACK ZIPES

PENGUIN BOOKS

PENGUIN BOOKS
Published by the Penguin Group
Penguin Group (USA) Inc., 375 Hudson Street, New York, New York 10014, U.S.A.
Penguin Group (Canada), 90 Eglinton Avenue East, Suite 700, Toronto, Ontario, Canada
M4P 2Y3 (a division of Pearson Penguin Canada Inc.)
Penguin Books Ltd, 80 Strand, London WC2R 0RL, England
Penguin Ireland, 25 St Stephen's Green, Dublin 2, Ireland
(a division of Penguin Books Ltd)
Penguin Group (Australia), 250 Camberwell Road, Camberwell, Victoria 3124, Australia
(a division of Pearson Australia Group Pty Ltd)
Penguin Books India Pvt Ltd, 11 Community Centre, Panchsheel Park,
New Delhi – 110 017, India
Penguin Group (NZ), 67 Apollo Drive, Rosedale, North Shore 0632, New Zealand
(a division of Pearson New Zealand Ltd)
Penguin Books (South Africa) (Pty) Ltd, 24 Sturdee Avenue, Rosebank,
Johannesburg 2196, South Africa

Penguin Books Ltd, Registered Offices: 80 Strand, London WC2R 0RL, England

The Story of a Puppet; or, the Adventures of Pinocchio, translated
by Mary Alice Murray published in Great Britain
by T. Fisher Unwin 1892
Revised translation by Giovanna Tassinari published in Great Britain by J. M. Dent &
Sons 1951
Edition with an afterword by Jack Zipes published
by Signet Books 1996
Published in Penguin Books 2002

5 7 9 10 8 6

Library of Congress Cataloging in Publication Data
Collodi, Carlo, 1826–1890.
[Avventure di Pinocchio. English]
Pinocchio : the tale of a puppet / by Carlo Collodi ; the original
translation by M.A. Murray ; revised by G. Tassinari ; illustrated by Charles
Folkard ; introduction by Jack Zipes.
p. cm.
Rev. translation originally published: Great Britain : J.M. Dent & Sons, 1951.
Summary: Pinocchio, a wooden puppet full of tricks and mischief, wants
more than anything else to become a real boy.
Includes bibliographical references.
ISBN 978-0-14-243706-3
[1. Fairy tales. 2. Puppets—Fiction.] I. Folkard, Charles, ill
II. Murray, M. A. (Mary Alice) III. Tassinari, G. (Giovanna) IV. Title.
PZ8.C7 Pi 2001
[Fic]—dc21   2001059335

Printed in the United States of America
Set in Stempel Garamond

CONTENTS

INTRODUCTION

If one were to believe Walt Disney's American film version of *Pinocchio* (1940), the wooden puppet turned human is a very happy boy at the end of his adventures. After numerous adventures, Pinocchio learns that honesty is the best policy, a message repeatedly driven home by Jiminy Cricket, the film's moral voice. Yet, the Italian novel of 1883 by Carlo Collodi is a much different affair. Pinocchio is indeed content to turn human at the end of this narrative, but there is a tragicomic element to the episodes that make one wonder why the puppet must endure so much suffering to become a proper and honest boy. Did Collodi intend to make an example out of Pinocchio, the good bad boy, who must learn to assume responsibility for his actions? Or, did he intend to show the harsh realities of peasant childhood in nineteenth-century Italy? Is Pinocchio perhaps a critical reflection of his own boyhood? After all, Carlo Collodi was not born into a well-endowed family, nor was he born with the name Collodi. His parents belonged to the Italian servant class, and the chances that he would become an important journalist and famous writer were slim. There was a fairy-tale element to his own education and development, and before we can fully understand why his Pinocchio, in contrast to Walt Disney's figure, is a tragicomic figure, we might do well to look at Collodi's life and times.

Born Carlo Lorenzini in Florence on November 24, 1826, Collodi was raised in a lower-class family with nine brothers and sisters. Living conditions were so poor that only two of his other siblings managed to survive childhood. His father and mother, Domenico and Angela Lorenzini, worked as servants for the Marquis Lorenzo Ginori, a wealthy aristocrat, who paid for Collodi's education. In fact, if it had not been for the Marquis Ginori's help, Collodi would never have gone to school. His parents were very poor, and they had so many children that Collodi, as the oldest, was sent to live with his grandparents in the little town of Collodi outside of Florence, where his mother was born. When he turned ten, the Marquis Ginori, acting as a kind of "fairy godfather," offered financial aid to send young Collodi to the seminary at Colle Val d'Elsa to study for the priesthood, but given his mischievous nature and dislike of monastic discipline, Collodi realized that he was not destined to be a priest. Therefore, by the time he was sixteen, Collodi began studying philosophy and rhetoric at the College of the Scolopi Fathers in Florence, and two years later, found a position at the Libreria Piatti, a leading bookstore, where he helped prepare catalogues for Giuseppe Aiazzi, one of the leading specialists for manuscripts in Italy. It was during this time that Collodi met numerous intellectuals and journalists and developed an interest in literature. By 1848, however, Collodi was carried away by patriotic zeal to fight for Italian independence against the Austrians. After the defeat of Italian forces that very same year, he was fortunate to obtain a position as a civil servant in the municipal government of Florence while also working as a journalist, editor, and dramatist. In 1853 he founded the satirical political magazine *Il Lampione* ("The Street Lamp") with the purpose of enlightening his compatriots about political oppression, but this publication was soon banned because his polemical writings were considered subversive by the Grand Duchy, loyal to the Austrian authorities. Not easily defeated, Collodi, started a second journal, *Lo Scaramuccia* ("The Controversy," 1854), which dealt more with theater and the arts than politics and lasted until 1858. Aside from publishing numerous articles, he also tried his hand at writing comedies, which did not have much success when they were produced. Indeed, he was more successful at politics and became known as an activist in liberal circles.

When the Second War of Independence erupted in 1859, Collodi volunteered for the cavalry, and this time, the Italians were victorious. Not only were the Austrians defeated in northern Italy, but the entire country was united under Giuseppe Garibaldi in 1861. It was during the period 1859–1861 that Collodi, still primarily known as Lorenzini, became involved in a dispute about Italian unification with Professor Eugenio Alberi of Pisa, a reputable political writer. In opposition to Alberi's negative position, he wrote a booklet defending the rise of a new Italy, and it was entitled, *Il signor Alberi ha ragione! Dialogo apologetico* (1860), and signed with the pseudonym Collodi in honor of his mother's native village, where he had spent his childhood. It was the first time he used this name not realizing that it would become world famous, mainly through the later publication of a children's book.

Though convinced that unification was positive for Italy, Collodi soon discovered that the social changes he had expected for all Italians were not about to take place. Instead, the nobility profited most from the defeat of the Austrians, and corruption continued in the government that supported the development of industry and the wealthy classes. He himself was fortunate since he was able to keep his position as a civil servant from 1860 to 1881 in the Commission of Theatrical Censorship and in the Prefecture of Florence. These appointments enabled him to serve as the stage director of the Teatro della Pergola in Florence and on the editorial committee that began research for an encyclopedia of the Florentine dialect. However, Collodi, who still wrote mainly under the name of Lorenzini, did not give up his career as journalist and freelance writer. In fact, he published a number of stories in *Io Fanfulla. Almanacco per il 1876* (1876) and in *Il Novelliere* (1876), which were reworked into sardonic sketches of Florentine life in *Macchiette* ("Sketches," 1879), the first book to be published under the pseudonym Collodi. In addition, he translated eighteenth-century French fairy tales by Charles Perrault, Mme. d'Aulnoy, and Mme. Le Prince de Beaumont under the title *I raconti delle fate* in 1876 and began reworking the didactic tales of the eighteenth-century Italian writer Parravinci in his book *Giannettino* ("Little Johnnie") in 1879, which led to a series: *Il viaggio per l'Italia* ("Little Johnnie's Travels through Italy," 1880), *La Grammatica di Giannettino* ("The Grammar of Little Johnnie," 1882), *L'abbaco di Giannettino* ("Little Johnnie's Book of Arithmetic," 1885), *La geografia di Giannettino* ("Little Johnnie's Geography," 1886), and others, all published as textbooks for elementary school children.

Collodi's fairy tale translations and textbooks prepared the way for his writing of *Pinocchio*, which was never really conceived as a book. Collodi was asked in the summer of 1881 by the editors of a weekly magazine for children, *Giornale per i bambini* ("Newspaper for Children") to write a series of stories, and he began the first installment in July of that year under the title of *Storia di un burattino* ("Story of a Puppet"). During the next two years Collodi continued to submit stories about Pinocchio to the magazine, and in 1883 they were gathered together in book form and published by Felice Paggi as *The Adventures of Pinocchio*.

Though the book was an immense success and went through four editions by the time he died in 1890, Collodi himself did not profit much from the publication due to the lack of good copyright laws protecting authors. The book was first translated into English in 1892 by Mary Alice Murray, and by the mid-twentieth century it had been printed in a hundred different languages, abridged, bowdlerized, parodied, and adapted for stage, film, and television. Such widespread popularity may be due to the fact that *Pinocchio* appears to be a symbolic narrative of boyhood that transcends its Italian origins and speaks to young and old about the successful rise of a ne'er-do-well. It is the consummate Horatio Alger story of the nineteenth century, a pull-yourself-up-by-the-bootstraps fairy tale, which demonstrates that even a log of wood has the potential to be good, human, and socially useful. Yet, it is also a story of punishment and conformity, a tale in which a puppet without strings has strings of social constraint attached so that he will not go his own way but respond to the pulls of superior forces, symbolized by the Blue Fairy and Geppetto. It is from the tension of the tragicomic that Pinocchio as a character lives and appeals to all audiences. Most important it is the fairy-tale structure which provides the episodes with the form and optimistic veneer and makes us forget how grueling and traumatic boyhood can be, especially boyhood in late nineteenth-century Italy.

Here it is important to remember the unique manner in which Collodi began *Pinocchio*:

Once upon a time there was . . .
'A king!' my young readers will instantly exclaim.
No, children, that's where you're wrong. Once upon a time there was a piece of wood!

This beginning indicates that Collodi, just like William Thackeray (*The Rose and the Ring*, 1855), Lewis Caroll (*Alice's Adventures in Wonderland*, 1865), and George MacDonald (*The Princess and the Goblin*, 1872), had been experimenting in England, was about to expand upon the fairy-tale tradition in a most innovative manner. Like Hans Christian Andersen, who had begun writing his unusual stories in 1835, Collodi fused genres based on the oral folk tale and the literary fairy tale to create his own magical land inhabited by bizarre creatures. By turning both genres and the real world upside down, he sought to question the social norms of his times and to interrogate the notion of boyhood.

In his use of folklore, Collodi consciously played with the worldwide tradition of "Jack tales," which generally deal with a naive well-intentioned lad, who, despite the fact that he is not too bright, manages to lead a charmed life and survives all sorts of dangerous encounters. Sometimes he becomes rich and successful at the end of the story. For the most part he is just content to return home safe and sound. In Italy there are numerous oral tales about bungling peasants, whose naiveté is a blessing and enables them to overcome difficulties in adventure after adventure. And, in Tuscany, the region in which Collodi grew up, there were many tales about Florentines such as the one told by Italo Calvino in *Italian Folktales* entitled "The Florentine," in which a young Florentine feels like a blockhead because he had never been away from Florence and never had any adventures to recount. After he leaves and travels about, however, he almost loses his life when he encounters a ruthless giant. Fortunately he escapes but loses a finger in the process. When he returns to Florence, he is cured of his urge to travel. What is significant in all the "Jack" tales, no matter what their country or region of origin, is that the essential "goodness" of the protagonist—that is, his good nature—protects him from evil forces, and in many cases, he learns to use his wits to trick his enemies who want to deceive or exploit him.

In the literary fairy-tale tradition of Europe, the "Jack" tales, so prominent among storytellers of all nations, are not very prevalent because literary fairy tales were generally first written for upper-class audiences and mainly for adults, and bungling peasant heroes were not of particular interest to the educated classes except as a topic for mockery. However, noses were, and Collodi knew about the noses from French fairy tales, some of which he had translated. For instance, in Charles Perrault's "The Foolish Wishes" (1697), a woodcutter's wife is cursed when her husband makes a bad wish and a sausage is attached to her nose. In Madame Leprince de Beaumont's "Prince Désir" (1757), a prince is born with a very long nose and compels everyone in his kingdom to think that long noses are the best in the world until an old fairy punishes him for his arrogance and vanity. Aside from noses, the donkey or ass was also familiar and appealing. The most famous example is Apuleius's *The Golden Ass*, written in the second century. It concerns Lucius, a young man, who is transformed into an ass because of his decadent life and must prove to the goddess Isis that he knows what mature love means before he can be changed back into a human being. There are numerous folk and fairy tales from Shakespeare's *A Midsummer Night's Dream* (1600) through Wilhelm Hauff's *Little Mook* (1827), in which a man is changed into a donkey as punishment for immoral or stupid behavior. The motifs of the unusual nose and the man transformed into an ass were obviously appealing to Collodi, but it was not just the nose or the donkey alone that made his narrative about *Pinocchio* so unique. Rather it his combination of the folklore and literary fairy-tale traditions to reflect upon the situation of illiterate playful poor boys during the latter half of the nineteenth century in Italy that make his narrative so compelling. Moreover, Collodi never wrote simply for an audience of young readers. His work was intended to appeal to children and adults and to suggest a mode of educating young boys, especially when they did not seem fit to be educated.

Read as a type of *Bildungsroman* or fairy-tale novel of development, *Pinocchio* can be interpreted positively as a representation of how peasant boys, when given a chance, can assume responsibility for themselves and their families and become industrious members of society and compassionate human beings. After all, Pinocchio is literally carved out of wood, out of an inanimate substance, and turns miraculously into a human boy, who becomes responsible for the welfare of his poor father. This theme of education or development, however, is very complex, for Collodi had not initially planned to allow Pinocchio to develop. In fact, he had intended to end the series printed in *Il giornale per i bambini* at Chapter Fifteen in which Pinocchio is left hanging on an oak tree, ostensibly dead. Yet, when this episode appeared in the November 10, 1881, issue of the newspaper with the word "finale" printed at the end, there was such a storm of protest from the readers, young and old, that Collodi was forced to resume Pinocchio's adventures in the February 16, 1882, issue of the newspaper. In other words, Collodi was forced to "develop" or "educate" his wooden protagonist despite his initial pessimistic perspective. Therefore, if the development of a piece of wood as a young boy is the central theme of *Pinocchio*, it is a theme that the author ironically questioned from the very beginning of the adventures, just as he questioned the optimistic structure of the fairy tale. This questioning accounts for the tension of skepticism and optimism in the novel. Moreover, the very structure of all the episodes also contributes to the tension because they were never designed to culminate in a novel, just as Pinocchio was never intended to become human. He was to serve as a negative example of what happens to a peasant boy who, when given the opportunity to advance in society, succumbs to the pleasure principle. The hanging in the November 1881 issue of *Il giornale per i bambini* was due punishment for Pinocchio's misbehavior and ignorance. Yet, as I have mentioned, the hanging was not allowed to last.

Collodi conceived each chapter for the newspaper to keep his readers interested in the strange fate of a "live" piece of wood that is turned into a puppet. He did this with irony and suspense. Though not predictable, each episode begins with a strange situation that leads to a near tragedy and borders on the ridiculous. However, since Collodi created a topsy turvy fairy-tale world that faintly resembled Tuscany but constantly changed shape, anything was possible, and Collodi mischievously played with the readers by leaving them hanging in suspense at the end of each chapter. Each episode is a predicament. And one predicament leads to the next. No chapter is ever finished. Even the end of the book can be considered "unfinished," for it is uncertain what lies ahead of Pinocchio after he turns human. He is still a boy. He has very little money. He is not educated. There is no indication that he will prosper as does the hero of a traditional fairy tale, even though he has developed a sense of responsibility and compassion. Pinocchio has survived boyhood and has been civilized to take the next step into manhood—and it is unclear where this step may lead.

Given the unfinished business of Pinocchio's development, Collodi's major and constant question throughout this fairy-tale novel of education is whether it is indeed worthwhile becoming "civilized." It is a question that Mark Twain was asking about the same time when he wrote *The Adventures of Huckleberry Finn* (1884), and in some ways Huck Finn is the American version of Pinocchio, for both boys are brutally exposed to the hypocrisy of society and yet compelled to adapt to the values and standards that will allegedly enable them to succeed. Huck refuses civilization in the end while Pinocchio appears to have made peace with law and order.

Yet, ultimately, Collodi asks us to consider how this socialization has come about, and if we consider how the innocent piece of wood, whose vices consist of his playfulness and naiveté, is treated by the people and social forces around him, then there is something tragic to the way he is beaten and lulled into submission. From the beginning, Pinocchio's origins are stamped by the fact that Geppetto carves him into a boy puppet because he wants to earn a living through the puppet. Simply put, his father "gives birth" to him because he wants to earn money through him. Geppetto has no interest in learning who his son is and what his desires are. His son is an investment in his own future. This is not to imply that Geppetto is an uncaring father, but his relationship to Pinocchio is ambivalent because of his initial desire to create a puppet that will know how to dance, fence, and turn somersaults so that he can earn a crust of bread and a glass of wine. In other words, Pinocchio is supposed to please him, and Geppetto literally holds the strings to the puppet's fate in his hands. In Chapter Seven, after Pinocchio has lost his feet, Geppetto at first refuses to make new feet for him until Pinocchio says, "I promise you, papa, that I will learn a trade, and that I will be the comfort and staff of your old age." Geppetto complies with Pinocchio's wish, and the puppet shows his gratitude by expressing his desire to go to school. In addition, he is extremely moved when Geppetto sells his own coat to purchase a spelling-book required for school. Collodi comments: "And Pinocchio, although he was very merry by nature, became sad also; because poverty, when it is real poverty, is understood by everybody—even by boys."

On the one hand, Pinocchio wants to be and is socialized to gratify his father; on the other, he cannot control his natural instincts to explore the world and to seek pleasure. Caught in a predicament—to please his father means to deny his own pleasures—Pinocchio as a poor illiterate peasant boy must learn the "ups and downs of the world," as Geppetto puts it; that is, he must be physically subdued and put in his place so that he functions properly as an industrious worker, curbed of his rebellious instincts. Collodi clearly demonstrates in a very specific class analysis that poor Italian boys of this period had very little choice if they wanted to advance in life. Using Pinocchio as a symbolic figure, Collodi torments and punishes the puppet each time Pinocchio veers from the norm of acceptable behavior. Among his punishments are the loss of legs through burning; the expansion of his nose due to lying; the hanging from an oak tree; imprisonment for four months; trapped and used by a farmer as a watchdog;

caught in a net and almost fried as a fish by the Green Fisherman; transformed into a donkey; compelled to work in a circus; drowned to escape skinning; and swallowed by a gigantic shark.

By no means was Collodi a sadist or different in his attitude toward educating children. He was very much a believer in "spare the rod, spoil the child." But he also took a sneaking delight in portraying that the punishment was out of proportion to the "crimes" committed by the young. In this respect, there is an interesting parallel that can be drawn with the most famous picture book for children of the nineteenth century, Heinrich Hoffmann's *Struwwelpeter* (*Slovenly Peter*, 1845), which consists of seven hilarious verse stories of warning. Without mincing words, each one of Hoffmann's illustrated tales tells children in graphic detail what will happen to them if they do not do as they are told. With the exception of the story about Pauline and the matches and another about the wild hunter, his witty verses all concern naughty boys who are severely punished for disobeying bourgeois rules of decency. Thus Frederick must lie in bed in pain while the dog that he mistreats gets to eat his sumptuous dinner. Conrad's thumbs are snipped off by the dreadful tailor because he cannot stop sucking them. Hans falls into a pond, loses his briefcase, and almost dies because he does not look where he is going. There is more cruelty in the verses, but the point here is that Hoffmann and Collodi were very representative of a general European attitude toward children and the importance of corporal punishment. Both supported rigorous moral training and unconsciously questioned it at the same time through the comic depictions of their good bad boys.

The forms of punishment in Collodi's novel are, of course, so preposterous that readers can take laugh at the events. The laughter, I believe, will also be mixed with relief that the readers do not have to undergo such tortures. Moreover, the laughter is instructive, for readers learn what to avoid through Pinocchio's mistakes and how to attain dignity. It is this attainment of self-dignity as a human being that is most crucial at the end of Pinocchio's adventures. As in most fairy-tale narratives, Pinocchio is obliged to fulfill specific tasks to gain his reward, and here two chores are primary: Pinocchio must first rescue his father Geppetto, and second he must keep his promises to the Blue Fairy by showing that he can be obedient, honest, and industrious. No matter how much he suffers, he perseveres and earns the recognition of the Blue

Fairy. He is also able to distinguish between good and bad, between ridiculous puppet and responsible boy behavior. In this regard, Collodi's narrative is a fairy-tale novel of development that makes a sober statement, despite its humor and grotesque scenes.

In his insightful study, *Adam and Eve and Pinocchio: On Being and Becoming Human*, the psychoanalyst Willard Gaylin uses the novel as a paradigm for explaining how a caring and living human being is created out of the narcissistic side of the infant. He focuses on the themes of dependency, work, conscience, and love to demonstrate how Pinocchio acquires human dignity through different learning experiences that enable him to understand how all his actions affect the people around him and his environment as well. By the end of the novel, that is, by the end of Pinocchio's learning process, he grasps that love is not narcissistic self-gratification, but it involves the deep pleasure of giving of one's self and contributes to the cohesive moral and civilizing force in human life.

For readers of Collodi's time, who were largely from the middle and educated classes, *Pinocchio* set a model of civilized behavior and sent a warning to mischievous scamps. Most importantly, the novel sought to make a distinction between ethical and unethical behavior. For Collodi himself, one can speculate that he viewed *Pinocchio* in part as representing the difficulties he himself experienced and had to overcome if he wanted to be accepted in Florentine society of his time, and this is a perspective that other readers from the lower classes may have had. For today's readers, Collodi's *Pinocchio* may come as a surprise, for most will probably be shocked to find that the novel is not the same as the Disney film which they have probably seen before reading Collodi's original work. They will realize that Collodi let his imagination run more wild than Disney did, and that he developed his puppet in more extraordinary ways with a serious intent to grasp and interrogate what it meant to "civilize" a child. Indeed, thanks to Collodi's wild imagination, we have a rich commentary on what it meant to develop as a peasant boy in Italian society of the nineteenth century. But more important, perhaps, his fairy-tale novel transcends questions of national identity and history and continues to raise questions about how we "civilize" children in uncivilized times.

SUGGESTIONS FOR FURTHER READING

Bacon, Martha. "Puppet's Progress: Pinocchio." In *Children and Literature: Views and Reviews*, ed. Virginia Havilland. Glenview, Illinois: 1973. 71–77.

Cambi, Franco. *Collodi, De Amicis, Rodari: Tre immagini d'infanzia.* Bari: edizioni Dedalo, 1985.

Cambon, Glauco. "Pinocchio and the Problem of Children's Literature." *Children's Literature* 2 (1973): 50–60.

Card, Claudia. "Pinocchio." In *From Mouse to Mermaid: The Politics of Film, Gender, and Culture*. Ed. Elizabeth Bell, Lynda Haas, and Laura Sells. Bloomington, Indiana: University of Indiana Press, 1995. 62–71.

"Carlo Collodi." *Children's Literature Review*, Ed. Gerald J. Senick. Detroit: Gale Research, 1983. 69–87.

Cech, John. "The Triumphant Transformation of Pinocchio." In *Triumphs of the Spirit in Children's Literature*. Ed. Francelia Butler and Richard Rotert. Hamden, CT: Library Professional Publishers, 1986. 171–77.

Cro, Stelio. "When Children's Literature Becomes Adult." *Merveilles et Contes* 7 (1993): 87–112.

Gannon, Susan R. "A Note on Collodi and Lucian." *Children's Literature* 8 (1980): 98–192.

———. "*Pinocchio*: The First Hundred Years." *Children's Literature Association Quarterly* 6 (Winter 1981/82): 1, 5–7.

Gaylin, Willard. *Adam and Eve and Pinocchio: On Being and Becoming Human*. New York: Viking, 1990.

Heins, Paul. "A Second Look: *The Adventures of Pinocchio*." *Horn Book Magazine* 58 (1982): 200–204.

Heisig, James W. "Pinocchio: Archetype of the Motherless Child." *Children's Literature* 3 (1974): 23–35.

Lucas, Ann Lawson, "Introduction" in *The Adventures of Pinocchio*. New York: Oxford University Press, 1996.

———. "Nations on Trial: The Cases of *Pinocchio* and *Alice*" in *Gunpowder and Sealing Wax: Nationhood in Children's Literature*. Ed. Ann Lawson Lucas. Market Harborough, England: Troubador, 1997.

———. "Enquiring Mind, Rebellious Spirit: Alice and Pinocchio as Nonmodel Children." *Children's Literature in Education* 30 (September 1999): 157–69.

Morrisey, Thomas J. "Alive and Well But Not Unscathed: A Response to Susan T. Gannon's '*Pinocchio*: The First Hundred Years.'" *Children's Literature Association Quarterly* 7 (Summer 1982): 37–39.

———. "Death and Rebirth in *Pinocchio*." *Children's Literature* 11 (1983): 64–75.

———. *Pinocchio Goes Modern: The Perils of a Puppet in the United States*. New York: Routledge, 2002.

Perella, Nicolas J. "An Essay on *Pinocchio*" in *The Adventures of Pinocchio: Story of a Puppet*, Trans. Nicolas J. Perella. Berkeley: University of California Press, 1986. 1–69.

Rodari, Gianni. "Pinocchio nella letteratura per l'infanzia." In *Studi Collodiani*. Pescia: Fondazione Nazionale Carlo Collodi, 1976. 37–57.

Rosenthal, M. L. "Alice, Huck, Pinocchio, and the Blue Fairy: Bodies Real and Imagined." *The Southern Review* 29 (Summer 1993): 486–90.

Teahan, James. T. "Introduction." In *The Pinocchio of C. Collodi*, Trs. James T. Teahan. New York: Schocken, 1985: pp. xv-xxx

———. "C. Collodi 1826–1890." In *Writers for Children: Critical Studies of Major Authors Since the Seventeeth Century*, Ed. Jane M. Bingham. New York: Charles Scribner's Sons, 1988: pp. 129–137.

Wunderlich, Richard and Thomas J. Morrisey. "The Desecration of *Pinocchio* in the United States." *The Horn Book Magazine* 58 (April 1982): 205–212.

———. "*Pinocchio* Before 1920: The Popular and the Pedagogical Traditions." *Italian Quarterly* 23 (Spring 1982): 61–72.

Wunderlich, Richard. *The Pinocchio Catalogue*. New York: Greenwood, 1988.

———. "De-Radicalizing *Pinocchio*." In *Functions of the Fantastic*, Ed. Joe Sanders. Westport: Greenwood Press, 1995: pp. 19–28.

Zago, Ester. "Carlo Collodi as Translator: From Fairy Tale to Folk Tale." *Lion and Unicorn* 12 (1988): 61–73.

A NOTE ON THE TEXT

This edition of *Pinocchio: The Tale of a Puppet* uses the translation by Mary Alice Murray (*The Story of a Puppet, or, The Adventures of Pinocchio*, 1892) revised by Giovana Tassinari (1951). The illustrations by Charles Folkard first appeared in a 1911 edition of Murray's translation.

PINOCCHIO

THE TALE OF A PUPPET

I

HOW IT CAME TO PASS THAT MASTER CHERRY THE CARPENTER FOUND A PIECE OF WOOD THAT LAUGHED AND CRIED LIKE A CHILD.

ONCE UPON A TIME there was . . .

'A king!' my young readers will instantly exclaim.

No, children, that's where you're wrong. Once upon a time there was a piece of wood!

It was not a grand piece of wood; it was only a common log, like one of those that you burn in winter-time in stoves and fireplaces, so as to make a cheerful blaze and to warm the rooms.

I cannot say how it came about, but the fact is, that one fine day this piece of wood was lying in the shop of an old carpenter by the name of Master Antonio. Everybody, however, called him Master Cherry, because the tip of his nose was always red and shining, like a ripe cherry.

No sooner had Master Cherry set eyes on the piece of wood

than his face beamed with delight; and, rubbing his hands together with satisfaction, he said softly to himself:

'This wood has come at the right moment; it will just do to
make the leg of a little table.'

Having said this he immediately took a sharp axe with which
to remove the bark and the rough surface. Just, however, as he
was going to give the first stroke he remained with his arm suspended in the air, for he heard a very small voice saying implor-
ingly: 'Don't strike me so hard!'

Just imagine what good old Master Cherry felt like!

He turned his terrified eyes all round the room to try and
discover where the little voice could possibly have come from,
but he saw nobody! He looked under the bench—nobody; he
looked into a cupboard that was always shut—nobody; he
looked into a basket of shavings and sawdust—nobody; he even
opened the door of the shop and gave a glance into the street—
and still nobody. Who, then, could it be?

'I see how it is,' he said, laughing and scratching his wig; 'evidently that little voice was all my imagination. Let's set to work
again.'

And taking up the axe he struck a tremendous blow on the
piece of wood.

'Oh! oh! you have hurt me!' cried the same little voice dole-
fully.

This time Master Cherry was petrified. His eyes started out
of his head with fear, his mouth opened, and his tongue hung out
almost to the end of his chin, so that he looked like a gargoyle.
As soon as he had recovered himself, he began to stutter, trembling all over with fear.

'But where on earth can that little voice that cried out "Oh!
oh!" have come from? There isn't a living soul here. Are you going to tell me that this piece of wood has learnt to cry and wail
like a child? I'm not going to believe that. Here it is, a piece of
wood, a log of fuel just like all the others, and if it were thrown
on to the fire it would just be enough to boil a pan of beans. Well
then? Can someone be hidden inside it? If there *is* someone hidden inside so much the worse for him! I'll settle him, once and
for all.'

So saying, he seized the poor piece of wood and began beating it without mercy against the walls of the room.

Then he stopped to listen if he could hear again the little wailing voice. He waited two minutes—nothing; five minutes—nothing; ten minutes—still nothing!

'I understand,' he said, trying to laugh and pushing his wig up; 'evidently the little voice that said "Oh! oh!" was all my imagination! Let's set to work again.'

All the same, he was terribly frightened, and he tried to sing to get up his courage.

Putting the axe aside he took up his plane so as to shape and polish the bit of wood, but while he was running it up and down he heard the same little voice, only this time it was laughing.

'Oh stop! You're tickling my tummy.'

This time poor Master Cherry fell down as if he had been struck by lightning. When at last he opened his eyes he found himself sitting on the floor.

His face was quite changed, and even the tip of his nose, instead of being crimson, had become blue with fright.

II

MASTER CHERRY MAKES A PRESENT OF THE PIECE OF WOOD TO HIS FRIEND GEPPETTO, WHO ACCEPTS IT BECAUSE HE PLANS TO MAKE A WONDERFUL PUPPET WHO WILL KNOW HOW TO DANCE, FENCE, AND TURN SOMERSAULTS.

AT THAT MOMENT there was a knock on the door.

'Come in,' said the carpenter, who had not the strength to rise to his feet.

A brisk little old man walked into the shop. His name was Geppetto, but when the boys of the neighbourhood wanted to make him wild they called him by the nickname of Polendina,[1] because of his yellow wig, which was just like porridge made from maize meal.

Geppetto was very fiery. Woe betide any one who called him Polendina. He would fly into a terrible temper, and there was no holding him.

'Good day, Master Antonio,' said Geppetto; 'what are you doing there on the floor?'

'I am teaching the alphabet to the ants.'

'Much good may that do you.'

---

[1]Polendina comes from polenda, or polenta, which is an Italian dish, very like porridge, but made from the flour of Indian corn, or maize meal.

'What has brought you to me, neighbour Geppetto?'

'My legs. But to say the truth, Master Antonio, I am come to ask a favour of you.'

'Here I am, ready to serve you,' replied the carpenter, rising on his knees.

'This morning an idea came into my head.'

'Let's hear it.'

'I have made up my mind to make myself a beautiful wooden puppet: a wonderful puppet that will know how to dance, fence, and turn somersaults. I want to go round the world with this puppet, so that I can earn a crust of bread and a glass of wine. How does it strike you?'

'Good for you, Polendina,' cried the same little voice which came from goodness knows where.

When he heard himself called Polendina Geppetto became as red as a pepper-plant with rage, and turning to the carpenter he said in a fury:

'Why are you insulting me?'

'Who's insulting you?'

'You've just called me Polendina.'

'It wasn't me!'

'Are you trying to tell me that it was me calling myself Polendina? I tell you it was you.'

'No!'

'Yes!'

'No!'

'Yes!'

And becoming angrier and angrier they came from words to blows, and seizing each other by the hair they bit and scratched and knocked each other about.

When the fight was over Master Antonio was in possession of Geppetto's yellow wig, and Geppetto discovered that the grey wig belonging to the carpenter had stuck between his teeth.

'Give me back my wig,' screamed Master Antonio.

'And you, give me back mine and let's be friends.'

The two old men having each recovered his own wig shook hands, and swore that they would remain friends to the end of their lives.

'Well then, neighbour Geppetto,' said the carpenter, to prove

When the fight was over . . .

that peace had been made, 'what is the favour that you want of me?'

'I want a little wood to make my puppet; will you give me some?'

Master Antonio was delighted, and he immediately went to the bench and fetched the piece of wood that had frightened him so much. But just as he was going to give it to his friend the piece of wood gave a shake, and wriggling violently out of his hands struck with all its force against the skinny shins of poor Geppetto.

'Ah, that's a nice way of giving a present, Master Antonio. You've almost lamed me.'

'I'll swear it wasn't me.'

'Was it me, then?'

'The wood is entirely to blame!'

'I know that it was the wood; but it was you who hit my legs with it!'

'I didn't hit you with it!'

'Liar!'

'Geppetto, don't insult me or I shall call you Polendina!'

'Ass!'

'Polendina!'

'Donkey!'

'Polendina!'

Geppetto returned to his home

'Baboon!'

'Polendina!'

On hearing himself called Polendina for the third time Geppetto, blind with rage, fell upon the carpenter and they fought desperately.

When the battle was over Master Antonio had two more scratches on his nose, and his adversary had two buttons the less on his waistcoat. Their accounts being thus squared they shook hands, and swore to remain good friends for the rest of their lives.

Geppetto carried off his fine piece of wood and, thanking Master Antonio, returned limping to his house.

III

GEPPETTO HAVING RETURNED HOME BEGINS AT ONCE TO MAKE A PUPPET, TO WHICH HE GIVES THE NAME OF PINOCCHIO. THE FIRST TRICKS PLAYED BY THE PUPPET.

GEPPETTO'S HOME was a little ground-floor room that got its light from a staircase. The furniture couldn't have been simpler: there was a poor chair, a bed that wasn't up to much, and a small, broken-down table. It's true that on the wall, facing the door, you could see a fire-place with a lighted fire; but the fire was a painted one, and by the side of the fire there was a saucepan, painted as well, boiling cheerfully and sending out a cloud of smoke just like real smoke.

As soon as he reached home Geppetto took his tools and set to work to cut out and model his puppet.

'What name shall I give him?' he said to himself; 'I think I shall call him Pinocchio. It is a name that will bring him luck. I once knew a whole family so called. There was Pinocchio the father, Pinocchia the mother, and Pinocchi the children, and all of them did well. The richest of the lot was a beggar.'

Having found a name for his puppet he began to work in good earnest, and he first made his hair, then his forehead, and then his eyes.

Having done the eyes, just think of his astonishment when he noticed that they could move and were looking straight at him.

Geppetto, finding himself stared at by those two wooden eyes, felt almost offended and said angrily:

'You naughty wooden eyes, why are you looking at me?'

No one answered.

He then proceeded to carve the nose; but no sooner had he made it than it began to grow. And it grew, and grew, and grew, until in a few minutes it had become an enormously long nose that seemed as if it would never end.

Poor Geppetto tired himself out with cutting it off; but the more he cut and shortened it the longer did that impertinent nose become!

The mouth was not even completed when it began to laugh and to mock at him.

'Stop laughing!' said Geppetto; but he might as well have spoken to the wall.

'Stop laughing, I say!' he roared in a threatening tone.

The mouth then ceased laughing, but put out its tongue as far as it would go.

Geppetto, not to spoil his handiwork, pretended not to see, and continued his work. After the mouth he fashioned the chin, then the throat, then the shoulders, the stomach, the arms, and the hands.

The hands were scarcely finished when Geppetto felt his wig snatched from his head. He turned round, and what did he see? He saw his yellow wig in the puppet's hand.

'Pinocchio! . . . Give me back my wig instantly!'

But Pinocchio, instead of returning it, put it on his own head, and nearly disappeared altogether.

Geppetto at this insolent and impudent behaviour felt sadder and more melancholy than he had ever been in his life before; and turning to Pinocchio he said to him:

'You young rascal! You're not yet finished, and you're already beginning to show lack of respect for your father! That is bad, my boy, very bad!'

And he dried a tear.

The legs and the feet had still to be done.

When Geppetto had finished the feet he received a kick on the tip of his nose.

'I deserve it!' he said to himself; 'I should have thought of it sooner! Now it is too late!'

He then took the puppet under the arms and placed him on the floor to teach him how to walk.

Pinocchio's legs were stiff and he could not move, but Geppetto led him by the hand and showed him how to put one foot before the other.

When his legs became flexible Pinocchio began to walk by himself and to run about the room; until, having gone out of the house door, he jumped into the street and escaped.

Poor Geppetto rushed after him but was not able to overtake him, for that rascal Pinocchio leapt in front of him like a hare, and knocking his wooden feet together against the pavement made as much clatter as twenty pairs of peasants' clogs.

'Stop him! stop him!' shouted Geppetto; but the people in the street, seeing a wooden puppet running like a racehorse, stood still in astonishment at the sight, and laughed, and laughed, and laughed, until their sides ached.

At last, as good luck would have it, a policeman appeared who, hearing the uproar, thought that a colt had escaped from his master. Planting himself courageously with his legs apart in the middle of the road he waited with the determined purpose of stopping him, and thus preventing the chance of worse disasters.

Geppetto rushed after him

When Pinocchio, still at some distance, saw the policeman blocking the whole street, he endeavoured to take him by surprise and to pass between his legs. But he failed dismally.

The policeman without stirring an inch caught him cleverly by the nose—it was an immense nose of ridiculous proportions that seemed made on purpose to be laid hold of by policemen— and consigned him to Geppetto, who had every intention of giving him a smart pull at the ears at once by way of punishment. Can you guess what he felt like when he couldn't find Pinocchio's ears, and do you know why? Because, in his hurry, he had forgotten to make him any ears.

So he seized him by the scruff of his neck, and as he was taking him back he shook his head threateningly and said:

'Let's go home, and as soon as we're there I promise you I'll get to the bottom of this.'

As soon as Pinocchio heard this he threw himself on the ground and refused to walk another step. In the meantime a crowd of idlers and busybodies began to form a ring round them.

Some of them said one thing, some another.

'Poor puppet!' said several, 'he is right not to want to go home! Who knows how Geppetto, that bad old man, will beat him!'

And the others added maliciously:

'Geppetto seems a good man, but with boys he is a regular tyrant! If that poor puppet is left in his hands he is quite capable of tearing him to pieces!'

At last they made such a fuss that it ended in the policeman setting Pinocchio at liberty and taking Geppetto to prison. The poor old man, taken by surprise, had no words in his own defence, and as he was being led away to jail he sobbed out:

'Wretched boy! To think of all the trouble I took to make him a nice puppet. It serves me right. I should have thought of it sooner.'

What happened afterwards is a story that really is past all belief, but I will relate it to you in the following chapters.

IV

THE STORY OF PINOCCHIO AND THE
TALKING CRICKET, FROM WHICH WE SEE
THAT NAUGHTY BOYS CANNOT BEAR TO BE
CORRECTED BY THOSE WHO KNOW
MORE THAN THEY DO.

WELL THEN, children, I must tell you that while poor Geppetto was being taken to prison for no fault of his, that imp Pinocchio, finding himself free from the clutches of the policeman, ran off as fast as his legs could carry him. So as to get home all the faster he rushed across the fields, and in his mad hurry he jumped high banks, thorn hedges, and ditches full of water, exactly as a kid or a young hare would have done if pursued by hunters.

Having arrived at the house he found the street door ajar. He pushed it open, went in, and having fastened the latch he threw himself down on the ground and gave a great sigh of satisfaction.

But his satisfaction did not last long, for he heard someone in the room who was saying:

'Cri-cri-cri!'

'Who's that?' said Pinocchio in a fright.

'It's me!'

Pinocchio turned round and saw a big cricket crawling slowly up the wall.

'Tell me, Cricket, who may you be?'

'I am the Talking Cricket, and I have lived in this room a hundred years and more.'

'Oh, it's my room now,' said the puppet, 'and you'd oblige

me very much by taking yourself off at once. Don't bother to look behind you.'

'I will not go from here,' answered the Cricket, 'until I have told you a great truth.'

'Tell it, then, and hurry up.'

'Woe to those boys who turn against their parents and run away from home for no reason whatever: they will never come to any good in this world, and sooner or later they will repent bitterly.'

'Sing away, my good Cricket, as much as you please. I've already made up my own mind to run away from here to-morrow at daybreak, because if I stay here they'll do to me the same as to all the other boys. They'll send me to school, and I'll have to study whether I want to or no. Between you and me I don't want to learn anything, it's much more amusing to chase butterflies and to climb trees so as to steal little birds from their nests.'

'You poor idiot! Don't you know that in that way you'll grow up an utter donkey and every one will make fun of you?'

'Shut up, you wicked old croaker!' shouted Pinocchio.

But the Cricket, who was patient and philosophical, instead of getting angry at such impertinence, went on in the same tone:

'If you don't like going to school then why not learn an honest trade, so that you can earn your own bread and butter?'

'Very well, I'll tell you,' answered Pinocchio, who was losing his patience. 'There's only one trade in the world that really takes my fancy.'

'And what trade would that be?'

'That's to eat, drink, and sleep, and to have a good time from morning till night—a regular idler's life!'

'You'd better know,' said the Talking Cricket in his calm way, 'that those who follow that trade end nearly always either in hospital or in prison.'

'Look out, you horrid old Cricket. If I fly into a temper it'll be the worse for you.'

'Poor Pinocchio! I really pity you!'

'Why do you pity me?'

'Because you are a puppet and, what is worse, because you have a wooden head.'

At these last words Pinocchio jumped up in a rage, and

Pinocchio ... snatching a wooden hammer ...

snatching a wooden hammer from the bench he threw it at the Talking Cricket.

Perhaps he never meant to hit him; but unfortunately it struck him exactly on the head, so that the poor Cricket had scarcely breath to cry cri-cri-cri, and then he stuck, flattened against the wall, stiff and lifeless.

V

PINOCCHIO IS HUNGRY AND LOOKS FOR AN EGG TO MAKE HIMSELF AN OMELETTE; BUT JUST AT THE MOST INTERESTING MOMENT THE OMELETTE FLIES OUT OF THE WINDOW.

NIGHT WAS COMING ON, and Pinocchio, remembering that he had eaten nothing all day, began to feel a gnawing in his stomach that was very like a good appetite.

But an appetite with boys grows quickly, and in fact after a few minutes his appetite had become hunger, and in no time at all his hunger became ravenous—a hunger that was really difficult to bear.

Poor Pinocchio ran quickly to the fire-place where a saucepan was boiling, and was going to take off the lid to see what was in it, but the saucepan was only painted on the wall. Just think what he felt like. His nose, which was already long, became longer by at least three inches.

Then he began to run about the room, searching in the drawers and in every imaginable place, in hopes of finding a bit of bread. If it were only a bit of dry bread, a crust, a bone left by a dog, a little mouldy pudding of Indian corn, a fish bone, a cherry stone—in fact anything that he could gnaw. But he could find nothing, nothing at all, absolutely nothing.

And in the meanwhile his hunger grew and grew; and poor Pinocchio had no other relief than yawning, and his yawns were such enormous ones that sometimes his mouth stretched to where his ears would have been, if he had had any. And after he had yawned he spluttered, and felt as if he was going to faint.

Then he began to cry bitterly, saying:

'The Talking Cricket was right. I did wrong to turn against my papa and to run away from home. . . . If my papa was here I should not now be dying of yawning! Oh, what a dreadful illness hunger is!'

Just then he thought he saw something in the dust-heap—something round and white that looked like a hen's egg. It took Pinocchio one moment to leap to it and seize it in his hand. It was indeed an egg.

Pinocchio's joy beats description; it can only be imagined. Almost believing it must be a dream he kept turning the egg over in his hands, feeling it, and kissing it. And as he kissed it he said:

'And now, how shall I cook it? Shall I make an omelette? . . . No, it would be better to cook it in a pannikin! . . . Or would it not be more savoury to fry it in the frying-pan? Or shall I simply boil it? No, the quickest way of all is to cook it in a pannikin: I am in such a hurry to eat it!'

Without loss of time he placed an earthenware pannikin on a brazier full of red-hot embers. Into the pannikin instead of oil or butter he poured a little water; and when the water began to smoke, tac! . . . he broke the egg-shell over it that the contents might drop in. But instead of the white and the yolk a gay little chicken popped out. It made Pinocchio a polite curtsy and said to him:

'A thousand thanks, Master Pinocchio, for saving me the trouble of breaking the shell. Good-bye until we meet again. Keep well, and give my best regards to every one!'

Thus saying it spread its wings, darted through the open window, and was lost to sight.

The poor puppet stood as if he had been stunned, with his eyes fixed, his mouth open, and the egg-shell in his hand. Recovering, however, from his first stupefaction, he began to cry and scream, and to stamp his feet on the floor in sheer despair, and amidst his sobs he said:

'Ah! how right the Talking Cricket was! If I had not run

Thus saying it spread its wings

away from home, and if my papa was here, I should not now be dying of hunger! Oh, what a dreadful illness hunger is!'

And as his inside was crying out for food more than ever, and he did not know how to quiet it, he thought he would leave the house and explore the neighbourhood in the hope of finding some charitable person who would give him a piece of bread.

VI

PINOCCHIO FALLS ASLEEP WITH HIS FEET ON THE BRAZIER, AND WAKES IN THE MORNING TO FIND THEM BURNT OFF.

IT WAS A WILD and stormy winter's night. The thunder was terrific and the lightning so vivid that the sky seemed on fire. A bitter blustering wind was whistling angrily, raising clouds of dust and making the trees creak and groan as it swept over the countryside.

Pinocchio was very much afraid of the thunder, but hunger was stronger than fear. He therefore closed the house door, and made a rush for the town, which he reached in a succession of leaps, with his tongue hanging out and panting for breath, like a setter after game.

But when he got there he found everything dark and deserted. The shops were closed, the windows and doors shut fast, and there wasn't so much as a dog in the streets. It seemed the land of the dead.

Pinocchio, urged by hunger and despair, seized hold of the bell of one of the houses and began to peal it with all his might, saying to himself:

'Someone ought to look out!'

Someone did. A little old man appeared at a window with a nightcap on his head, and called to him angrily:

'What do you want at this time of night?'

'Would you be kind enough to give me a little bread?'

'Wait there, I'll be back directly,' said the little old man,

It was a wild and stormy winter's night

thinking he had to do with one of those rascally boys who amuse themselves at night by ringing the house bells of respectable people who are sleeping soundly.

After a minute the window was again opened, and the voice of the same little old man shouted to Pinocchio:

'Come underneath and hold out your cap.'

Pinocchio pulled off his cap; but just as he held it out an enormous basin of water was poured down on him, watering him from head to foot as if he had been a pot of dried-up geraniums.

He returned home like a wet chicken quite exhausted with fatigue and hunger; and having no longer the strength to stand he sat down and rested his damp and muddy feet on a brazier full of burning embers.

And then he fell asleep; and whilst he slept his feet, which were wooden, caught fire, and little by little they burnt away and became cinders.

Pinocchio continued to sleep and to snore as if his feet be-

Whilst he slept his feet ... caught fire

longed to someone else. At last about daybreak he awoke because someone was knocking at the door.

'Who's there?' he asked, yawning and rubbing his eyes.

'It's me!' answered a voice.

And the voice was Geppetto's voice.

VII

GEPPETTO RETURNS HOME, MAKES THE PUPPET NEW FEET, AND GIVES HIM THE BREAKFAST THAT THE POOR MAN HAD BROUGHT FOR HIMSELF.

POOR PINOCCHIO, whose eyes were still half closed with sleep, had not as yet discovered that his feet were burnt off. The moment, therefore, that he heard his father's voice he slipped off his stool to run and open the door; but after stumbling two or three times he fell his whole length on the floor.

And the noise he made in falling was as if a sack of wooden ladles had been thrown from a fifth-floor window.

'Open the door!' shouted Geppetto from the street.

'Dear papa, I can't,' answered the puppet, crying and rolling about on the ground.

'Why can't you?'

'Because my feet have been eaten.'

'And who has eaten your feet?'

'The cat,' said Pinocchio, seeing the cat, who was having fun, playing with some shavings on the floor.

'Open the door, I tell you!' repeated Geppetto. 'If you don't, when I get into the house I'll give you to the cat right enough!'

'I can't stand up, believe me. Oh, poor me! poor me! I shall have to walk on my knees for the rest of my life!'

Geppetto, believing that all this lamentation was only another of the puppet's tricks, thought of a means of putting an end to it, and climbing up the wall he got in at the window.

He was very angry, and at first he did nothing but scold; but when he saw his Pinocchio lying on the ground and really with-

'Oh, poor me! poor me!   I shall have to walk on my knees
for the rest of my life!'

out feet he was quite overcome. He took him in his arms and began to kiss him and to make a fuss of him, and as the big tears ran
down his cheeks, he sobbed:

'My little Pinocchio! how did you manage to burn your
feet?'

'I don't know, papa, but believe me it has been an infernal
night that I shall remember as long as I live. It thundered and
lightened, and I was very hungry, and then the Talking Cricket
said to me: "It serves you right; you have been wicked and you
deserve it," and I said to him: "Take care, Cricket!" . . . and he
said: "You are a puppet and you have a wooden head," and I
threw a hammer at him, and he died, but the fault was his, for I
didn't wish to kill him, and the proof of it is that I put an earthenware pannikin on a brazier of burning embers, but a chicken flew
out and said: "Good-bye until we meet again, and best regards to
every one," and I got still more hungry, for which reason that little old man in a nightcap opening the window said to me: "Come
underneath and hold out your hat," and poured a basinful of water on my head, but asking for a little bread isn't a disgrace, is it?
and I returned home at once, and because I was so very hungry I
put my feet on the brazier to dry them, and then you returned,

and I found they were burnt off, and I am so hungry, but I have no longer any feet! Oh! oh! oh! oh!' And poor Pinocchio began to cry and to roar so loudly that he could be heard five miles off.

Geppetto, who from all this jumbled account had only understood one thing, which was that the puppet was dying of hunger, drew from his pocket three pears, and giving them to him said:

'These three pears were meant for my breakfast; but I will give them to you willingly. Eat them, and I hope they'll do you good.'

'If you wish me to eat them be kind enough to peel them for me.'

'Peel them?' said Geppetto, astonished. 'I should never have thought, my boy, that you were so dainty and fastidious. That is bad! In this world we should accustom ourselves from childhood to like and to eat everything, for there is no saying what may happen to us. There are so many ups and downs in this world!'

'I cannot bear rind'

'You are no doubt right,' interrupted Pinocchio, 'but I will never eat fruit that has not been peeled. I cannot bear rind.'

So that good Geppetto fetched a knife, and arming himself with patience peeled the three pears, and put the rind on a corner of the table.

Having eaten the first pear in two mouthfuls, Pinocchio was about to throw away the core; but Geppetto caught hold of his arm and said to him:

'Do not throw it away; in this world everything may be of use.'

'I'm not going to eat the core!' shouted the puppet, turning upon him like a viper.

'Who knows? there are so many ups and downs in this world!' repeated Geppetto without losing his temper.

And so the three cores, instead of being thrown out of the window, were placed on the corner of the table, together with the three rinds.

Having eaten, or rather having devoured the three pears, Pinocchio yawned tremendously, and then said in a fretful tone:

'I am as hungry as ever!'

'But, my boy, I have nothing more to give you!'

'Nothing, really nothing?'

'I have only the rind and the cores of the three pears.'

'I must have patience!' said Pinocchio; 'if there is nothing else I will eat a rind.'

And he began to chew it. At first he made a wry face; but then one after another he quickly disposed of the rinds, and after the rinds even the cores, and when he had eaten up everything he clapped his hands on his sides in his satisfaction, and said joyfully:

'Ah! now I feel comfortable.'

'You see now,' observed Geppetto, 'that I was right when I said to you that it did not do to let ourselves be too particular or too dainty in our tastes. We can never know, my dear boy, what may happen to us. There are so many ups and downs in this world!'

VIII

GEPPETTO MAKES PINOCCHIO NEW FEET
AND SELLS HIS OWN COAT TO BUY HIM
A SPELLING-BOOK.

NO SOONER had the puppet appeased his hunger than he began to cry and to grumble because he wanted a pair of new feet.

But Geppetto, to punish him for his naughtiness, allowed him to cry and to groan for half the day. Then he said to him:

'Why should I make you new feet? To make it easy for you, perhaps, to run away from home again?'

'I promise you,' said the puppet, sobbing, 'that for the future I will be good.'

'All boys,' replied Geppetto, 'when they are bent upon getting something, say the same thing.'

'I promise you that I will go to school, and that I will study and do well.'

'All boys, when they are bent on getting something, tell the same story.'

'But I am not like other boys! I am the best of all boys, and I always speak the truth. I promise you, papa, that I will learn a trade, and that I will be the comfort and the staff of your old age.'

Geppetto, although he tried to look so stern, had his eyes full of tears and his heart full of sorrow at seeing his poor Pinocchio in such a pitiable state. He did not say another word, but taking his tools and two small pieces of well-seasoned wood he set to work in real earnest.

In less than an hour the feet were finished: two little feet—swift, well-knit, and full of energy. They might have been modelled by an artist of genius.

Geppetto then said to the puppet:

'Shut your eyes and go to sleep!'

And Pinocchio shut his eyes and pretended to be asleep.

And whilst he pretended to sleep Geppetto, with a little glue which he had melted in an egg-shell, fastened his feet in their place, and it was so well done that not even a trace could be seen of where they were joined.

No sooner had the puppet discovered that he had feet than he jumped down from the table on which he was lying, and began to spring and to cut a thousand capers about the room, as if he had gone mad with delight.

'To reward you for what you have done for me,' said Pinocchio to his father, 'I will go to school at once.'

'Good boy.'

'But if I'm to go to school I shall need some clothes.'

Geppetto, who was poor, and who had not so much as a farthing in his pocket, then made him a little dress of flowered paper, a pair of shoes from the bark of a tree, and a cap of bread-crumbs kneaded into a dough.

Pinocchio ran immediately to look at himself in a basin of water, and he was so pleased with his appearance that he said, strutting about like a peacock:

'I look quite like a gentleman!'

'Yes, indeed,' answered Geppetto, 'for bear in mind that it is not fine clothes that make the gentleman, but rather it is clean clothes.'

'By the by,' added the puppet, 'to go to school I am still in want—indeed I am without the best thing, and the most important.'

'And what is it?'

'I have no spelling-book.'

'You are right: but what shall we do to get one?'

'It is quite easy. We have only to go to the bookseller's and buy it.'

'And the money?'

'I have got none.'

'No more have I,' added the good old man very sadly.

And Pinocchio, although he was very merry by nature, became sad also; because poverty, when it is real poverty, is understood by everybody—even by boys.

Ran to look at himself in a crock of water

'Well, patience!' exclaimed Geppetto, all at once rising to his feet, and putting on his old fustian coat, all patched and darned, he ran out of the house.

He returned shortly, holding in his hand a spelling-book for Pinocchio, but the old coat was gone. The poor man was in his shirt-sleeves, and out of doors it was snowing.

'And the coat, papa?'

'I have sold it.'

'Why did you sell it?'

'Because I found it too hot.'

Pinocchio understood this answer in an instant, and unable to restrain the impulse of his good heart he sprang up, and, throwing his arms round Geppetto's neck, he hugged him again and again.

IX

PINOCCHIO SELLS HIS SPELLING-BOOK IN ORDER THAT HE MAY GO AND SEE A PUPPET-SHOW.

As soon as it had done snowing Pinocchio set out for school with his fine spelling-book under his arm. As he went along he began to imagine a thousand things in his little brain, and to build a thousand castles in the air, one more beautiful than the other.

And talking to himself he said:

'To-day at school I will learn to read at once; then to-morrow I will begin to write, and the day after tomorrow to learn numbers. Then with my acquirements I will earn a great deal of money, and with the first money I have in my pocket I will immediately buy for my papa a beautiful new cloth coat. But what am I saying? Cloth, indeed! It shall be all made of gold and silver, and it shall have diamond buttons. That poor man really deserves it; for to buy me books and have me taught he has remained in his shirt-sleeves. . . . And in this cold! It is only fathers who are capable of such sacrifices!'

Whilst he was saying this with great emotion he thought that he heard music in the distance that sounded like fifes and the beating of a big drum: fi-fi-fi, fi-fi-fi, zum, zum, zum, zum.

He stopped and listened. The sounds came from the end of a cross street that led to a little village on the seashore.

'What can that music be? What a pity that I have to go to school, or else . . .'

And he remained irresolute. It was, however, necessary to

He heard . . . the beating of a big drum

come to a decision. Should he go to school? or should he go after the fifes?

'To-day I will go and hear the fifes, and to-morrow I will go to school,' finally decided the young scape-grace, shrugging his shoulders.

The more he ran the nearer came the sounds of the fifes and the beating of the big drum: fi-fi-fi, zum, zum, zum, zum.

At last he found himself in the middle of a square quite full of people, who were all crowding round a building made of wood and canvas, and painted a thousand colours.

'What is that building?' asked Pinocchio, turning to a little boy who belonged to the place.

'Read the placard—it is all written—and then you will know.'

'I would read it willingly, but it so happens that to-day I don't know how to read.'

'Bravo, blockhead! Then I will read it to you. The writing on that placard in those letters red as fire is:

'GREAT PUPPET THEATRE'

'Has the play begun long?'
'It is beginning now.'
'How much does it cost to go in?'
'Twopence.'

Pinocchio, who was in a fever of curiosity, lost all control of himself, and without any shame he said to the little boy to whom he was talking:

'Would you lend me twopence until to-morrow?'

'I would lend them to you willingly,' said the other, taking him off, 'but it so happens that to-day I cannot give them to you.'

'I will sell you my jacket for twopence,' the puppet then said to him.

'What do you think that I could do with a jacket of flowered paper? If it rained and it got wet it would be impossible to get it off my back.'

The book was sold there and then

'Will you buy my shoes?'

'They would only be of use to light the fire.'

'How much will you give me for my cap?'

'That would be a wonderful bargain indeed! A cap made of bread! There would be a risk of the mice coming to eat it whilst it was on my head.'

Pinocchio was on thorns. He was on the point of making another offer, but he had not the courage. He hesitated, felt irresolute and remorseful. At last he said:

'Will you give me twopence for this new spelling-book?'

'I am a boy and I don't buy from boys,' replied the other, who had much more sense than Pinocchio had.

'I will buy the spelling-book for twopence,' called out a hawker of old clothes, who had been listening to the conversation.

And the book was sold there and then. And to think that poor Geppetto had remained at home trembling with cold in his shirt sleeves, that he might buy his son a spelling-book!

X

THE PUPPETS RECOGNIZE THEIR BROTHER PINOCCHIO, AND RECEIVE HIM WITH DELIGHT; BUT AT THAT MOMENT THEIR MASTER FIRE-EATER MAKES HIS APPEARANCE AND PINOCCHIO IS IN DANGER OF COMING TO A BAD END.

WHEN PINOCCHIO CAME into the little puppet theatre something happened that nearly provoked a riot.

You must know that the curtain was up, and that the play had already begun.

Harlequin and Punchinello were on the stage, quarrelling with each other as usual, and threatening to come to blows at any moment.

The audience were all ears, laughing until their sides ached as they listened to the bickering of those two puppets who gesticulated and called each other names so naturally that they might indeed have been two real human beings, belonging to this world.

All at once Harlequin stopped short, and turning to the audience he pointed to the back of the pit and cried dramatically:

'Heavens above! Am I dreaming or waking? Surely that's Pinocchio down there!'

'It is indeed Pinocchio!' cried Punchinello.

The audience were . . . laughing until their sides ached

'It is Pinocchio himself!' screamed Rosaura, the lady puppet, peeping out at the back of the stage.

'It's Pinocchio! It's Pinocchio!' cried all the puppets in chorus, jumping out from behind the scenes. 'It's Pinocchio! It's our brother Pinocchio! Long live Pinocchio!'

'Come up here to me, Pinocchio,' cried Harlequin. 'Come and throw yourself into the arms of your wooden brothers.'

At this affectionate invitation Pinocchio leapt from the back of the pit into the stalls; with another leap he poised on the head of the conductor of the orchestra, and then he sprang on to the stage.

It's hard to describe, in the midst of the hubbub that fol-

They carried him in triumph in front of the footlights

lowed, the embraces, the hugs, the friendly pinches, and the demonstrations of warm, brotherly affection, in the way of wooden heads banging against his, that Pinocchio received from the excited actors and actresses of the puppet dramatic company.

The sight was doubtless a moving one, but the audience, finding that the play had stopped, became impatient, and began to shout: 'We want the play—go on with the play!'

It was all breath thrown away. The puppets, instead of going on with the play, redoubled their noise and outcries, and putting

Pinocchio on their shoulders they carried him in triumph in front of the footlights.

At that moment out came the showman. He was very big, and so ugly that the sight of him was enough to frighten any one. His beard was as black as ink, and so long that it reached from his chin to the ground. It's enough to say that he trod upon it when he walked. His mouth was as big as an oven, and his eyes were like two lanterns of red glass with lights burning inside them. He carried a large whip made of snakes and foxes' tails twisted together, which he cracked constantly.

At his unexpected appearance there fell a sudden silence; no one dared to breathe. You could have heard a fly buzz in the stillness. The poor puppets of both sexes trembled like so many leaves.

'Why have you come to make trouble in my theatre?' asked the showman of Pinocchio, in the terrible voice of an ogre with a bad cold in his head.

'Believe me, Your Honour, it was not my fault!'

'That's enough! I'll fix you later.'

As soon as the play was over the showman went into the kitchen where a fine sheep, preparing for his supper, was turning slowly on the spit in front of the fire. As there was not enough wood to finish roasting and browning it he called Harlequin and Punchinello, and said to them:

'Bring that puppet here: you will find him hanging on a nail. It seems to me that he is made of very dry wood, and I am sure that if he was thrown on the fire he would make a beautiful blaze for the roast.'

At first Harlequin and Punchinello hesitated; but, appalled by a severe glance from their master, they obeyed. In a short time they returned to the kitchen carrying poor Pinocchio, who was wriggling like an eel out of water, and screaming desperately: 'Papa! papa! save me! . . . I don't want to die! I don't want to die!'

XI

FIRE-EATER SNEEZES AND PARDONS
PINOCCHIO, WHO THEN SAVES THE LIFE OF
HIS FRIEND HARLEQUIN.

THE SHOWMAN'S NAME was Fire-eater, and it must be admitted that he looked simply frightful, especially because of his great black beard that covered his chest, and the whole of his legs, just like an apron, but at heart he wasn't really such a bad man. When he actually saw poor Pinocchio brought before him, struggling and screaming 'I don't want to die! I don't want to die!' he began to feel sorry for him. He tried to hold out, but after a little he could stand it no longer and he sneezed violently. When he heard the sneeze, Harlequin, who up to that moment had been in the deepest affliction, and bowed down like a weeping willow, became quite cheerful, and leaning towards Pinocchio he whispered to him softly:

'Good news, brother. The showman has sneezed, and that is a sign that he is sorry for you, and you are saved.'

For you must know that whilst most men, when they feel compassion for someone, either weep or at least pretend to wipe their eyes, Fire-eater, on the contrary, whenever he was really overcome, had the habit of sneezing. It was one way, like another, of showing that he had a heart.

After he had sneezed the showman, still pretending to be angry, shouted at Pinocchio:

'Stop crying! Your lamentations have given me a funny feel-

36

ing here in my tummy. . . . I feel such a pain that I almost . . . a-tchoo! a-tchoo!' and he sneezed again twice.

'Bless you!' said Pinocchio.

'Thank you! What about your papa and your mamma? Are they still alive?'

'My papa is! I never knew my mamma.'

'How sorry your poor old father would be if I had you thrown on to those burning coals! Poor old man! I feel for him . . . a-tchoo, a-tchoo, a-tchoo!' and he sneezed three times.

'Bless you!' said Pinocchio.

'Thank you! All the same I deserve some pity as well, for as you see I have no more wood with which to finish roasting my mutton, and to tell you the truth, in the circumstances you would have been very useful to me. However, I have had pity on you, so I must have patience. Instead of you I'll burn one of the other puppets of my company. Ho there, police!'

At this call two wooden policemen immediately appeared. They were very long and very thin, and had on cocked hats, and held naked swords in their hands.

The showman said to them in a gruff voice:

'Take Harlequin, bind him securely, and then throw him on the fire to burn. I am determined that my mutton shall be well roasted.'

Just think of poor Harlequin! His terror was so great that his legs bent under him, and he fell with his face on the ground.

At this agonizing sight Pinocchio, weeping bitterly, threw himself at the showman's feet, and bathing his long beard with his tears he began to say in a supplicating voice:

'Have pity, Mr. Fire-eater!'

'There are no misters here,' the showman answered harshly.

'Have pity, Sir Knight!'

'There are no knights here.'

'Have pity, Noble Lord!'

'There are no lords here.'

'Have pity, Your Excellency!'

On hearing himself called 'Your Excellency' the showman began to smile, and became at once kinder and more tractable. Turning to Pinocchio he asked:

'Well, what do you want from me?'

He sneezed three times

'I implore you to spare poor Harlequin.'

'There can be no mercy here. As I have spared you I must throw him on to the fire because I'm determined to have my mutton well roasted.'

'In that case,' cried Pinocchio proudly, rising to his feet, and throwing away his bread cap, 'in that case I know my duty. Come, policemen! Bind me and throw me to the flames. No, it is not right that poor Harlequin, my true friend, should die for me!'

These words, pronounced in a loud heroic voice, made all the puppets who were present cry. Even the policemen, although they were made of wood, wept like two newly born lambs.

Fire-eater at first remained as hard and unmoved as ice, but little by little he began to melt and to sneeze. And having sneezed four or five times he opened his arms affectionately, and said to Pinocchio:

'You are a good, brave boy! Come here and give me a kiss.'

Pinocchio ran at once, and climbing like a squirrel up the

Pinocchio . . . threw himself at the showman's feet

showman's beard he gave him a hearty kiss on the end of his nose.

'Then the pardon is granted?' asked poor Harlequin in a faint voice that was scarcely audible.

'The pardon is granted!' answered Fire-eater; he then added, sighing and shaking his head:

'I must have patience! To-night I shall have to resign myself to eat the mutton half raw; but another time, woe to him whose turn it shall be!'

At the news of the pardon the puppets all ran to the stage, and having lighted the lamps and chandeliers as if for a full-dress performance, they began to clap and to dance merrily. At dawn they were still dancing.

XII

THE SHOWMAN, FIRE-EATER, MAKES PINOCCHIO A PRESENT OF FIVE GOLD PIECES TO TAKE HOME TO HIS FATHER, GEPPETTO; BUT PINOCCHIO INSTEAD ALLOWS HIMSELF TO BE TAKEN IN BY THE FOX AND THE CAT, AND GOES WITH THEM.

THE FOLLOWING DAY Fire-eater called Pinocchio on one side and asked him:

'What is your father's name?'

'Geppetto.'

'And what trade does he follow?'

'That of a poor man.'

'Does he earn much?'

'Earn much? Why, he has never a penny in his pocket. Only think, to buy a spelling-book for me to go to school he was obliged to sell the only coat he had to wear—a coat that, between patches and darns, was not fit to be seen.'

'Poor devil! I feel almost sorry for him! Here are five gold pieces. Go at once and take them to him with my compliments.'

You can easily understand that Pinocchio thanked the showman a thousand times. He embraced all the puppets of the company one by one, even to the policemen, and beside himself with delight set out to return home.

But he had not gone far when he met on the road a Fox lame of one foot, and a Cat blind of both eyes, who were going along helping each other like good companions in misfortune. The Fox, who was lame, walked leaning on the Cat, and the Cat, who was blind, was guided by the Fox.

'Good day, Pinocchio,' said the Fox, accosting him politely.

'How do you come to know my name?' asked the puppet.

'I know your father well.'

'Where did you see him?'

'I saw him yesterday at the door of his house.'

'And what was he doing?'

'He was in his shirt-sleeves and shivering with cold.'

'Poor papa! But that is over; for the future he shall shiver no more!'

'Why?'

'Because I am a rich man now!'

'You a rich man!' said the Fox, and he began to laugh rudely and scornfully. The Cat also began to laugh, but to conceal it she combed her whiskers with her forepaws.

'There is little to laugh at,' cried Pinocchio angrily. 'I am really sorry to make your mouths water, but if you know anything about it you can see that these here are five gold pieces.'

And he pulled out the money that Fire-eater had made him a present of.

At the pleasant jingle of money the Fox, with an involuntary movement, stretched out the paw that had seemed crippled, and the Cat opened wide two eyes that looked like two green lanterns. It is true that she shut them again, and so quickly that Pinocchio observed nothing.

'And now,' asked the Fox, 'what are you going to do with all that money?'

'First of all,' answered the puppet, 'I intend to buy a new coat for my papa, made of gold and silver, and with diamond buttons; and then I will buy a spelling-book for myself.'

'For yourself?'

'Yes indeed: for I wish to go to school to study in earnest.'

'Look at me!' said the Fox. 'Through my foolish passion for study I have lost a leg.'

'Don't listen to the advice of bad companions'

'Look at me!' said the Cat. 'Through my foolish passion for study I have lost the sight of both my eyes.'

At that moment a white Blackbird, that was perched on the hedge by the road, began his usual song, and said:

'Pinocchio, don't listen to the advice of bad companions: if you do you will be sorry!'

Poor Blackbird! If only he had not spoken! The Cat, with a great leap, sprang upon him, and without even giving him time to say 'Oh!' ate him in a mouthful, feathers and all.

Having eaten him and cleaned her mouth she shut her eyes again and feigned blindness as before.

'Poor Blackbird!' said Pinocchio to the Cat. 'Why did you treat him so badly?'

'I did it to give him a lesson. He'll know better another time than to meddle in other people's conversation.'

They had gone almost half-way when the Fox, halting suddenly, said to the puppet:

'Would you like to double your money?'

'In what way?'

'Would you like to make out of your five miserable gold pieces a hundred, a thousand, two thousand?'

'I should think so! but how?'

'The way is easy enough. Instead of returning home you must go with us.'

'And where do you wish to take me?'

'To the land of the Owls.'

Pinocchio reflected a moment, and then he said resolutely:

'No, I will not go. I am already close to the house, and I will return home to my papa who is waiting for me. Who can tell how often the poor old man must have sighed yesterday when I did not come back? I have indeed been a bad son, and the Talking Cricket was right when he said: "Disobedient boys never come to any good in the world." I have found it to my cost, for many misfortunes have happened to me. Even yesterday in Fire-eater's house I ran the risk. . . . Oh! it makes me shudder only to think of it!'

'Well, then,' said the Fox, 'you are quite decided to go home? Go, then, and so much the worse for you.'

'So much the worse for you!' repeated the Cat.

'Think well of it, Pinocchio, for you are giving a kick to fortune.'

'To fortune!' repeated the Cat.

'Between to-day and to-morrow your five gold pieces would have become two thousand.'

'Two thousand!' repeated the Cat.

'But how is it possible that they could have become so many?' asked Pinocchio, remaining with his mouth open from astonishment.

'I will explain it to you at once,' said the Fox. 'You must know that in the land of the Owls there is a sacred field called by

everybody the Field of Miracles. In this field you must dig a little hole, and you put into it, we will say, one gold piece. You
then cover up the hole with a little earth: you must water it with
two pails of water from the fountain, then sprinkle it with two
pinches of salt, and when night comes you can go quietly to bed.
In the meanwhile, during the night, the gold piece will grow and
flower, and in the morning when you get up and return to the
field what do you find? You find a beautiful tree laden with as
many gold pieces as a fine ear of corn is laden with grains in the
month of June.'

'So that,' said Pinocchio, more and more bewildered, 'supposing I buried my five gold pieces in that field, how many
should I find there the following morning?'

'That is an exceedingly easy calculation,' replied the Fox, 'a
calculation that you can make on your fingers. Put that every
coin gives you an increase of five hundred: multiply five hundred
by five, and the following morning will find you with two thousand five hundred shining gold pieces in your pocket.'

'Oh! how delightful!' cried Pinocchio, dancing for joy. 'As
soon as ever I have obtained those gold pieces I will keep two
thousand for myself, and the other five hundred I will make a
present of to you two.'

'A present to us?' cried the Fox with indignation and ap-
pearing much offended. 'What are you dreaming of?'

'What are you dreaming of?' repeated the Cat.

'We do not work,' said the Fox, 'for vulgar interest: we work
solely to enrich others.'

'Others!' repeated the Cat.

'What good people!' thought Pinocchio to himself: and forgetting there and then his papa, the new coat, the spelling-book,
and all his good resolutions, he said to the Fox and the Cat:

'Let us be off at once. I will go with you.'

XIII

The inn of the Red Crayfish.

THEY WALKED, and walked, and walked, until at last, towards evening, they arrived dead tired at the inn of the Red Crayfish.

'Let us stop here a little,' said the Fox, 'that we may have something to eat and rest ourselves for an hour or two. We will start again at midnight so as to arrive at the Field of Miracles by dawn to-morrow morning.'

Having gone into the inn they all three sat down to table: but none of them had any appetite.

The Cat, who was suffering from indigestion and feeling seriously indisposed, could only eat thirty-five mullet with tomato sauce, and four portions of tripe with Parmesan cheese; and because she thought the tripe was not seasoned enough she asked three times for the butter and grated cheese!

The Fox would also willingly have picked a little, but as his doctor had ordered him a strict diet he was forced to content himself simply with a hare dressed with a sweet-sour sauce, and garnished lightly with fat chickens and early pullets. After the hare he sent for a special dish of partridges, rabbits, frogs, lizards, and other delicacies; he could not touch anything else. He had such an aversion to food, he said, that he could put nothing to his lips.

The one who ate the least was Pinocchio. He asked for some

walnuts and a hunch of bread, and left everything on his plate.
The poor boy, whose thoughts were continually fixed on the
Field of Miracles, had got an indigestion of gold pieces in ad-
vance.

When they had supped the Fox said to the host:

'Give us two good rooms, one for Mr. Pinocchio, and the
other for me and my companion. We will snatch a little sleep before we leave. Remember, however, that at midnight we wish to
be called to continue our journey.'

'Yes, gentlemen,' answered the host, and he winked at the
Fox and the Cat, as much as to say: 'I know what you are up to.
We understand one another!'

No sooner had Pinocchio got into bed than he fell asleep at
once and began to dream. And he dreamt that he was in the middle of a field, and the field was full of shrubs covered with clusters of gold pieces, and as they swung in the wind they went
clink, clink, clink, as much as to say: 'Let who will come and take
us.' But when Pinocchio was at the most interesting moment,
that is, just as he was stretching out his hand to pick handfuls of
those beautiful gold pieces, and to put them in his pocket, he was
suddenly wakened by three violent blows on the door of his
room.

It was the host who had come to tell him that midnight had
struck.

'Are my companions ready?' asked the puppet.

'Ready! Why, they left two hours ago.'

'Why were they in such a hurry?'

'Because the Cat had received a message to say that her eld-
est kitten was ill with chilblains on his feet and was in danger of
death.'

'Did they pay for the supper?'

'What are you thinking of? They are much too well brought
up to dream of offering such an insult to a gentleman like you.'

'What a pity! It is an insult that would have given me so
much pleasure!' said Pinocchio, scratching his head. He then
asked:

'And where did my good friends say they would wait
for me?'

He dreamt . . . of shrubs covered with clusters of gold pieces

'At the Field of Miracles, to-morrow morning at daybreak.'

Pinocchio paid a gold piece for his supper and that of his companions, and then left.

Outside the inn it was so pitch dark that he had almost to grope his way, for it was impossible to see a hand's breadth in front of him. In the surrounding country not a leaf was stirring. Only some night-birds flying across the road from one hedge to the other brushed Pinocchio's nose with their wings as they passed, which caused him so much terror that, springing back, he shouted: 'Who goes there?' and the echo in the surrounding hills repeated in the distance: 'Who goes there? Who goes there? Who goes there?'

As he was walking along he saw a little insect shining dimly on the trunk of a tree, like a nightlight in a lamp of transparent china.

'Who are you?' asked Pinocchio.

'I am the ghost of the Talking Cricket,' answered the insect in a low voice, so weak and faint that it seemed to come from the other world.

'What do you want with me?' said the puppet.

'I want to give you some advice. Go back, and take the four gold pieces that you have left to your poor father, who is weeping and in despair because you have never returned to him.'

'By to-morrow my papa will be a rich man, for these four gold pieces will have become two thousand.'

'Don't trust, my boy, to those who promise to make you rich in a day. Usually they are either mad or rogues! Give ear to me and go back.'

'On the contrary, I am determined to go on.'

'The hour is late!'

'I'm going on!'

'The night is dark!'

'I'm going on!'

'The road is dangerous!'

'I'm going on!'

'Remember that boys who are bent on having their own way and on pleasing themselves are sorry for it, sooner or later.'

'The same old tarradiddle! Good night, Cricket.'

'Good night, Pinocchio, and may Heaven preserve you from all dangers and from assassins!'

No sooner had he spoken these words than the Talking Cricket vanished suddenly, just as if a light had been blown out, and the road was darker than ever before.

XIV

Pinocchio falls amongst assassins because he would not heed the good advice of the Talking Cricket.

'Really,' said the puppet to himself as he resumed his journey, 'we poor boys are indeed unlucky! Every one scolds us, every one keeps on warning us, every one gives us good advice. To hear them talk they'd all take it into their heads to be our fathers and mothers; every one of them—even Talking Crickets. See here, just because I wouldn't listen to that tiresome Cricket, who knows how many misfortunes are to happen to me, according to him! I am even to meet with assassins! It's just as well that I don't believe in assassins, and that I never have believed in them. For my part I think that assassins have been purposely invented by papas to frighten boys who want to go out at night. Besides, even if I were to come across them here in this road, do you suppose I'd let them scare me? Not for a moment. I would go forward to meet them, crying out: "Assassins, my fine gentlemen, what do you want of me? You'd better remember that there's no joking with me. Go about your own business and keep quiet." At these words, spoken in a firm tone, those poor assassins—I see them now—would run away like the wind. If, however, they were so badly brought up as not to run away at once I would run away myself, and that would be the end of it. . . .'

But Pinocchio was not given the time to go on thinking, for in that moment he seemed to hear a rustle of leaves behind him.

He turned to look, and saw in the gloom two evil-looking black figures completely enveloped in charcoal sacks. They were running after him on tiptoe, and making great leaps like two phantoms.

'Here they are in reality!' he said to himself, and not knowing where to hide his gold pieces he put them in his mouth just under this tongue.

Then he tried to escape. But he had not gone a step when he felt himself seized by the arm, and heard two horrid sepulchral voices saying to him:

'Your money or your life!'

Pinocchio, not being able to answer in words, owing to the money that was in his mouth, made a thousand low bows, and by an elaborate display of dumb show tried to convey to those two muffled figures, whose eyes alone were visible through the holes in their sacks, that he was only a poor puppet, without as much as a false farthing in his pocket.

'Come now! Less nonsense and out with the money!' cried the two brigands threateningly.

But the puppet made a gesture with his head and his hands, as much as to say: 'I haven't got any.'

'Give up the money or you're a dead man!' said the taller of the brigands.

'Dead!' repeated the other.

'And after we have killed you we'll kill your father!'

'Your father too!'

'No, no, no, not my poor papa!' cried Pinocchio in a despairing tone; and as he said it the gold pieces clinked in his mouth.

'Ah! you rascal! Then you have hidden your money under your tongue! Spit it out at once!'

But Pinocchio was obstinate.

'Ah, you'd like to make out you're deaf, would you? Wait a bit, we'll find a way of making you spit it out.'

And one of them seized the puppet by the end of his nose, and the other took him by the chin, and began to pull them brutally, the one up and the other down, to force him to open his mouth. But it was all to no purpose. Pinocchio's mouth seemed to be nailed and riveted together.

**The puppet made a gesture with his head and his hands, as
much as to say: 'I haven't got any'**

Then the shorter assassin drew out an ugly knife and tried to
force it between his lips like a lever or chisel. But Pinocchio, as
quick as lightning, caught his hand with his teeth, and with one
bite bit it clean off and spat it out. Imagine his astonishment
when instead of a hand he perceived that he had spat a cat's paw
on to the ground.

Encouraged by this first victory he used his nails to such
purpose that he succeeded in liberating himself from his as-
sailants, and jumping the hedge by the roadside he began to fly
across country. The assassins ran after him like two dogs chasing
a hare: and the one who had lost a paw ran on three legs, and no
one ever knew how he managed to keep up.

After a race of some miles Pinocchio could do no more. Giving himself up for lost he climbed the trunk of a very high pine-
tree and seated himself in the top-most branches. The assassins
attempted to climb after him, but when they had reached half-
way up the stem they slid down again, and arrived on the ground
with the skin grazed from their hands and knees.

But they were not to be beaten by so little: collecting a quan-
tity of dry wood they piled it beneath the pine and set fire to it.
In less time than it takes to tell the pine began to burn and to
flame like a candle blown by the wind. Pinocchio, seeing that the
flames were mounting higher every instant, and not wishing to
end his life like a roasted pigeon, made a stupendous leap from
the top of the tree and started afresh across the fields and vine-

yards. The assassins followed him, and kept behind him without once giving in.

The day began to break and they were still pursuing him. Suddenly Pinocchio found his way barred by a wide deep ditch full of dirty water the colour of coffee. What was he to do? 'One! two! three!' cried the puppet, and making a rush he sprang to the other side. The assassins also jumped, but not having measured the distance properly—splash, splash! . . . they fell into the very middle of the ditch. Pinocchio, who heard the plunge and the splashing of the water, shouted out, laughing, and without stopping:

'A fine bath to you, assassins.'

And he felt convinced that they were drowned, until, turning to look, he perceived that on the contrary they were both running after him, still enveloped in their sacks, with the water dripping from them as if they had been two hollow baskets.

XV

THE ASSASSINS PURSUE PINOCCHIO; AND
HAVING OVERTAKEN HIM HANG HIM TO A
BRANCH OF THE BIG OAK.

AT THIS SIGHT the puppet's courage failed him, and he was on the point of throwing himself on the ground and giving himself up for lost. Turning, however, his eyes in every direction, he saw at some distance, standing out amidst the dark green of the trees, a small house as white as snow.

'If I had only breath to reach that house,' he said to himself, 'perhaps I should be saved.'

And without delaying an instant he began again running for his life through the wood, with the assassins after him.

At last, after a desperate race of nearly two hours, he arrived quite breathless at the door of the house, and knocked.

No one answered.

He knocked again with great violence, for he heard the sound of steps approaching him, and the heavy panting of his tormentors. The same silence.

Seeing that knocking was useless he began in desperation to kick and to beat his head against it. At that a lovely little girl came to the window. She had blue hair and a face as white as wax, but her eyes were closed, and her hands were crossed on her breast. Without moving her lips in the least she said in a soft little voice that seemed to come from another world:

'There is no one in this house. They are all dead!'

'Come and open the door to me yourself!' cried Pinocchio, weeping and entreating.

'I am dead too!'

'If I had only breath to reach that house,' he said

'Dead? then what are you doing there at the window?'

'I am waiting for the hearse to come to carry me away.'

Having said this she immediately disappeared, and the window was closed again without the slightest noise.

'Oh! beautiful Little Girl with blue hair,' cried Pinocchio, 'open the door for pity's sake! Have compassion on a poor boy pursued by assas——'

But he could not finish the word, for he felt himself seized by the collar, and the same two horrible voices said to him threateningly:

'You shall not escape from us again!'

The puppet, seeing death staring him in the face, was taken with such a violent fit of trembling that the joints of his wooden legs began to creak, and the gold pieces hidden under his tongue to clink.

'Now then,' demanded the assassins, 'will you open your mouth, yes or no? Ah! no answer? . . . Leave it to us: this time we will force you to open it! . . .'

And drawing out two long horrid knives as sharp as razors, clash . . . they attempted to stab him twice.

But the puppet, luckily for him, was made of very hard wood; the knives therefore broke into a thousand pieces, and the assassins were left with the handles in their hands staring at each other.

'I see what we must do,' said one of them. 'He must be hanged! let us hang him!'

'Let us hang him!' repeated the other.

Without loss of time they tied his arms behind him, passed a running noose round his throat, and then hanged him to the branch of a tree called the Big Oak.

They then sat down on the grass and waited for his last struggle. But at the end of three hours the puppet's eyes were still open, his mouth closed, and he was kicking more than ever.

Losing patience they turned to Pinocchio and said in a bantering tone:

'Good-bye till to-morrow. Let us hope that when we return you will be civil enough to allow yourself to be found quite dead, and with your mouth wide open.'

And they walked off.

In the meantime a tempestuous northerly wind began to blow and roar angrily, and it beat the poor puppet as he hung, making him swing violently from side to side like the clapper of a bell ringing for a wedding. And the swinging gave him atrocious spasms, and the running noose, becoming still tighter round his throat, took away his breath.

Little by little his eyes began to grow dim, but although he felt that death was near he still continued to hope that some charitable person would come to his assistance before it was too late. But when, after waiting and waiting, he found that no one came, absolutely no one, then he remembered his poor father, and thinking he was dying . . . he stammered out:

'Oh, papa! papa! if only you were here!'

His breath failed him and he could say no more. He shut his eyes, opened his mouth, stretched his legs, gave a long shudder, and hung there, stiff and unconscious.

XVI

THE LOVELY LITTLE GIRL WITH THE BLUE HAIR HAS THE PUPPET CUT DOWN; SHE HAS HIM PUT TO BED AND CALLS IN THREE DOCTORS TO KNOW IF HE IS ALIVE OR DEAD.

WHILST POOR PINOCCHIO, suspended to a branch of the Big Oak, was apparently more dead than alive, the lovely Little Girl with blue hair came again to the window. When she saw the unhappy puppet hanging by his throat, and dancing up and down in the gusts of the north wind, she was moved by compassion. Striking her hands together she made three little claps.

At this signal there came a sound of the sweep of wings flying rapidly, and a large Falcon flew on to the window-sill.

'What are your orders, gracious Fairy?' he asked, inclining his beak in sign of reverence—for I must tell you that the Little Girl with blue hair was no more and no less than a beautiful Fairy, who for more than a thousand years had lived in the wood.

'Do you see that puppet dangling from a branch of the Big Oak?'

'I see him.'

'Very well. Fly there at once: with your strong beak break the knot that keeps him suspended in the air, and lay him gently on the grass at the foot of the tree.'

The Falcon flew away, and after two minutes he returned, saying:

'I have done as you commanded.'

'And how did you find him?'

'At first sight he appeared dead, but he cannot really be quite dead, for I had no sooner loosened the running noose that tightened his throat than, giving a sigh, he muttered in a faint voice: "Now I feel better!" '

The Fairy then striking her hands together made two little claps, and a magnificent Poodle appeared, walking upright on his hind legs exactly as if he had been a man.

He was in the full-dress livery of a coachman. On his head he had a three-cornered cap braided with gold, his curly white wig came down on to his shoulders, he had a chocolate-coloured waistcoat with diamond buttons, and two large pockets to contain the bones that his mistress gave him at dinner. He had besides a pair of short crimson velvet breeches, silk stockings, low shoes, and hanging behind him a species of umbrella-case made of blue satin in which to put his tail when the weather was rainy.

'Be quick, Medoro, like a good dog!' said the Fairy to the Poodle. 'Bring out the most beautiful carriage in my coach-house, and take the road to the wood. When you come to the Big Oak you will find a poor puppet stretched on the grass half dead. Pick him up gently, and lay him flat on the cushions of the carriage and bring him here to me. Have you understood?'

The Poodle, to show that he had understood, wagged the blue satin cover on his tail three or four times, and ran off like a racehorse.

Shortly afterwards a beautiful little carriage came out of the coach-house. The cushions were stuffed with canary feathers, and it was lined in the inside with whipped cream, custard, and sponge cakes. The little carriage was drawn by a hundred pairs of white mice, and the Poodle, seated on the coach-box, cracked his whip from side to side like a driver when he is afraid that he is behind time.

A quarter of an hour had not passed when the carriage returned. The Fairy, who was waiting at the door of the house, took the poor puppet in her arms, and carried him into a little room that was wainscoted with mother-of-pearl, and sent at once to summon the most famous doctors in the neighborhood.

A magnificent Poodle appeared

The doctors came immediately one after the other: namely a Crow, an Owl, and a Talking Cricket.

'I wish to know from you gentlemen,' said the Fairy, turning to the three doctors who were assembled round Pinocchio's bed— 'I wish to know from you gentlemen if this unfortunate puppet is alive or dead.'

At this request the Crow, advancing first, felt Pinocchio's pulse; he then felt his nose, and then the little toe of his foot: and having done this carefully he pronounced solemnly the following words:

'To my belief the puppet is already quite dead; but if unfortunately he should not be dead then it would be a sign that he is still alive!'

'I regret,' said the Owl, 'to be obliged to contradict the Crow, my illustrious friend and colleague; but in my opinion the puppet is still alive: but if unfortunately he should not be alive then it would be a sign that he is dead indeed!'

'And you—have you nothing to say?' asked the Fairy of the Talking Cricket.

'In my opinion the wisest thing a prudent doctor can do, when he does not know what he is talking about, is to be silent. For the rest, that puppet there has a face that is not new to me. I have known him for some time. . . .'

Pinocchio, who up to that moment had lain immovable, like a real piece of wood, was seized with a fit of convulsive trembling that shook the whole bed.

'That puppet there,' continued the Talking Cricket, 'is a confirmed rogue. . . .'

Pinocchio opened his eyes, but shut them again immediately.

'He is a ragamuffin, a ne'er-do-well, a vagabond. . . .'

Pinocchio hid his face beneath the clothes.

'That puppet there is a disobedient son who will make his poor father die of a broken heart! . . .'

At that instant a suffocated sound of sobs and crying was heard in the room. Imagine everybody's astonishment when, having raised the sheets a little, they discovered that the sounds came from Pinocchio.

'When the dead person cries it is a sign that he is on the road to get well,' said the Crow solemnly.

'I grieve to contradict my illustrious friend and colleague,' added the Owl; 'but for me, when the dead person cries it is a sign that he is sorry to die.'

XVII

PINOCCHIO EATS THE SUGAR, BUT WILL
NOT TAKE HIS MEDICINE: WHEN,
HOWEVER, HE SEES THE GRAVE-DIGGERS,
WHO HAVE ARRIVED TO CARRY HIM AWAY,
HE TAKES IT. HE THEN TELLS A LIE,
AND AS A PUNISHMENT HIS NOSE
GROWS LONGER.

AS SOON as the three doctors had left the room the Fairy approached Pinocchio, and having touched his forehead she perceived that he was in a high fever that was not to be trifled with.

She therefore dissolved a certain white powder in half a tumbler of water, and offering it to the puppet she said to him lovingly:

'Drink it, and in a few days you will be cured.'

Pinocchio looked at the tumbler, made a wry face, and then asked in a plaintive voice:

'Is it sweet or bitter?'

'It is bitter, but it will do you good.'

'If it is bitter I will not take it.'

'Listen to me: drink it.'

'I don't like anything bitter.'

'Drink it, and when you have drunk it I will give you a lump of sugar to take away the taste.'

'Where is the lump of sugar?'

'Here it is,' said the Fairy, taking a piece from a gold sugar-basin.

'Give me first the lump of sugar, and then I will drink that bad bitter water.'

'Do you promise me?'

'Yes.'

The Fairy gave him the sugar, and Pinocchio, having crunched it up and swallowed it in a second, said, licking his lips:

'It would be a fine thing if sugar was medicine! I would take it every day.'

'Now keep your promise and drink these few drops of water, which will restore you to health.'

Pinocchio took the tumbler unwillingly in his hand, and put the point of his nose to it: he then approached it to his lips: he then again put his nose to it, and at last said:

'It is too bitter! too bitter! I cannot drink it.'

'How can you say that when you have not even tasted it?'

'I can imagine it! I know it from the smell. I want first another lump of sugar . . . and then I will drink it!'

The Fairy then, with all the patience of a good mamma, put another lump of sugar in his mouth, and then again presented the tumbler to him.

'I cannot drink it so!' said the puppet, making a thousand grimaces.

'Why?'

'Because that pillow down there at my feet bothers me.'

The Fairy removed the pillow.

'It is useless. Even so I cannot drink it.'

'What is the matter now?'

'The door of the room, which is half open, bothers me.'

The Fairy went and closed the door.

'In short,' cried Pinocchio, bursting into tears, 'I will not drink that bitter water—no, no, no!'

'My boy, you will repent it.'

'I don't care.'

'Your illness is serious.'

'I don't care.'

'The fever in a few hours will carry you into the other world.'

'I don't care.'

'Are you not afraid of death?'

'I am not in the least afraid! . . . I would rather die than drink that bitter medicine.'

At that moment the door of the room flew open, and four rabbits as black as ink entered carrying on their shoulders a little bier.

'What do you want with me?' cried Pinocchio, sitting up in bed in a great fright.

'We are come to take you,' said the biggest rabbit.

'To take me? . . . But I am not dead yet!'

'No, not yet: but you have only a few minutes to live, as you have refused the medicine that would have cured you of the fever.'

'Oh, Fairy, Fairy!' the puppet then began to scream, 'give me the tumbler at once . . . be quick, for pity's sake, for I will not die—no . . . I will not die.'

And taking the tumbler in both hands he emptied it at a draught.

'We must have patience!' said the rabbits; 'this time we have made our journey in vain.' And taking the little bier again on their shoulders they left the room, grumbling and muttering between their teeth.

In fact, a few minutes afterwards Pinocchio jumped down from the bed quite well: because you must know that wooden puppets have the privilege of being seldom ill and of being cured very quickly.

The Fairy, seeing him running and rushing about the room as gay and as lively as a young rooster, said to him:

'Then my medicine has really done you good?'

'Good, I should think so! It has restored me to life!'

'Then why on earth did you require so much persuasion to take it?'

'Because you see that we boys are all like that! We are more afraid of medicine than of the illness.'

'Disgraceful! Boys ought to know that a good remedy taken in time may save them from a serious illness, and perhaps even from death.'

'Oh! but another time I shan't require so much persuasion. I shall remember those black rabbits with the bier on their shoulders, and then I shall immediately take the tumbler in my hand, and down it will go!'

'Now come here to me, and tell me how it came about that you fell into the hands of those assassins.'

'It came about that the showman Fire-eater gave me some gold pieces and said to me: "Go, and take them to your father!" and instead I met on the road a Fox and a Cat, two very respectable persons, who said to me: "Would you like those pieces of gold to become a thousand or two? Come with us and we will take you to the Field of Miracles," and I said: "Let us go." And they said: "Let us stop at the inn of the Red Crayfish," and after midnight they left. And when I awoke I found that they were no longer there, because they had gone away. Then I began to travel by night, for you cannot imagine how dark it was: and on that account I met on the road two assassins in charcoal sacks who said to me: "Out with your money," and I said to them: "I have got none," because I had hidden the four gold pieces in my mouth, and one of the assassins tried to put his hand in my mouth, and I bit his hand off and spat it out, but instead of a hand I spat out a cat's paw. And the assassins ran after me, and I ran, and ran, until at last they caught me, and tied me by the neck to a tree in this wood, and said to me: "To-morrow we shall return here, and then you will be dead with your mouth open, and we shall be able to carry off the pieces of gold that you have hidden under your tongue."'

'And the four pieces—where have you put them?' asked the Fairy.

'I have lost them!' said Pinocchio; but he was telling a lie, for he had them in his pocket.

He had scarcely told the lie when his nose, which was already long, grew at once two inches longer.

'And where did you lose them?'

'In the wood near here.'

At this second lie his nose went on growing.

'If you have lost them in the wood near here,' said the Fairy, 'we will look for them, and we shall find them: because everything that is lost in that wood is always found.'

'Ah! now I remember all about it,' replied the puppet, getting quite confused; 'I didn't lose the four gold pieces, I swallowed them by accident whilst I was drinking your medicine.'

At this third lie his nose grew to such an extraordinary

His nose grew to such an extraordinary length . . .

length that poor Pinocchio could not move in any direction. If he turned to one side he struck his nose against the bed or the window-panes, if he turned to the other he struck it against the walls or the door, if he raised his head a little he ran the risk of sticking it into one of the Fairy's eyes.

And the Fairy looked at him and laughed.

'What are you laughing at?' asked the puppet, very confused and anxious at finding his nose growing so prodigiously.

'I am laughing at the lie you have told.'

'And how can you possibly know that I have told a lie?'

'Lies, my dear boy, are found out immediately, because they are of two sorts. There are lies that have short legs, and lies that have long noses. Your lie, as it happens, is one of those that have a long nose.'

Pinocchio, not knowing where to hide himself for shame, tried to run out of the room; but he did not succeed, for his nose had increased so much that it could no longer pass through the door.

XVIII

PINOCCHIO MEETS AGAIN THE FOX AND THE CAT, AND GOES WITH THEM TO BURY HIS MONEY IN THE FIELD OF MIRACLES.

THE FAIRY, as you can imagine, allowed the puppet to cry and to roar for a good half-hour over his nose, which could no longer pass through the door of the room. This she did to give him a severe lesson, and to correct him of the disgraceful fault of telling lies—the most disgraceful fault that a boy can have. But when she saw him quite disfigured, and his eyes swollen out of his head from weeping, she felt full of compassion for him. She therefore clapped her hands, and at that signal a thousand large birds called Woodpeckers flew in at the window. They immediately perched on Pinocchio's nose and began to peck at it with such zeal that in a few minutes his enormous and ridiculous nose was reduced to its usual dimensions.

'What a good Fairy you are,' said the puppet, drying his eyes, 'and how much I love you!'

'I love you also,' answered the Fairy; 'and if you will remain with me you shall be my little brother and I will be your good little sister.'

'I would remain willingly . . . but my poor papa?'

'I have thought of everything. I have already let your father know, and he will be here to-night.'

'Really?' shouted Pinocchio, jumping for joy. 'Then, little Fairy, if you consent I should like to go and meet him. I am so anxious to give a kiss to that poor old man, who has suffered so much on my account, that I am counting the minutes.'

'Go, then, but be careful not to lose yourself. Take the road through the wood and I am sure that you will meet him.'

Pinocchio set out; and as soon as he was in the wood he began to run like a young goat. But when he had reached a certain spot, almost in front of the Big Oak, he stopped, because he thought that he heard people amongst the bushes. In fact, two persons came out on to the road. Can you guess who they were? . . . His two travelling companions, the Fox and the Cat, with whom he had supped at the inn of the Red Crayfish.

'Why, here is our dear Pinocchio!' cried the Fox, kissing and embracing him. 'How come you to be here?'

'How come you to be here?' repeated the Cat.

'It's a long story,' answered the puppet, 'and I'll tell you when I have time. But do you know that the other night, when you left me alone at the inn, I met with assassins on the road——'

'Assassins! . . . Oh, poor Pinocchio! And what did they want?'

'They wanted to rob me of my gold pieces.'

'Villains!' said the Fox.

'Infamous villains!' repeated the Cat.

'But I ran away from them,' continued the puppet, 'and they followed me: and at last they overtook me and hung me to a branch of that oak-tree.'

And Pinocchio pointed to the Big Oak, which was two steps from them.

'Is it possible to hear of anything more dreadful?' said the Fox. 'In what a world we are condemned to live! Where can respectable people like us find a safe refuge?'

Whilst they were thus talking Pinocchio observed that the Cat was lame of her front right leg, for in fact she had lost her paw with all its claws. He therefore asked her:

'What have you done with your paw?'

The Cat tried to answer but became confused. Therefore the Fox said immediately:

'My friend is too modest, and that is why she doesn't speak.

'Why, here is our dear Pinocchio!' cried the Fox

I will answer for her. I must tell you that an hour ago we met an old wolf on the road, almost fainting from want of food, who asked alms of us. Not having so much as a fish-bone to give him, what did my friend, who has really a heart of gold, do? She bit off one of her forepaws, and threw it to that poor beast that he might appease his hunger.'

And the Fox, in relating this, dried a tear.

Pinocchio was also touched, and approaching the Cat he whispered into her ear:

'If all cats resembled you how fortunate the mice would be!'

'And now, what are you doing here?' asked the Fox of the puppet.

'I am waiting for my papa, whom I expect to arrive every moment.'

'And your gold pieces?'

'I have got them in my pocket, all but one that I spent at the inn of the Red Crayfish.'

'And to think that, instead of four pieces, by tomorrow they might become one or two thousand! Why do you not listen to my advice? why will you not go and bury them in the Field of Miracles?'

'To-day is impossible: I will go another day.'

'Another day it will be too late!' said the Fox.

'Why?'

'Because the field has been bought by a nobleman, and after to-morrow no one will be allowed to bury money there.'

'How far off is the Field of Miracles?'

'Not two miles. Will you come with us? In half an hour you will be there. You can bury your money at once, and in a few minutes you will collect two thousand, and this evening you will return with your pockets full. Will you come with us?'

Pinocchio thought of the good Fairy, old Geppetto, and the warnings of the Talking Cricket, and he hesitated a little before answering. He ended, however, by doing as all boys do who have not a grain of sense and who have no heart—he ended by giving his head a little shake, and saying to the Fox and the Cat:

'Let us go: I will come with you.'

And they went.

After having walked half the day they reached a town that was called Booby Town. As soon as Pinocchio entered this town he saw that the streets were crowded with dogs who had lost their coats and who were yawning from hunger, shorn sheep trembling with cold, cocks without combs or crests who were begging for a grain of Indian corn, large butterflies who could no longer fly because they had sold their beautiful coloured wings, peacocks who had no tails and were ashamed to be seen, and pheasants who went scratching about in a subdued fashion, mourning for their brilliant gold and silver feathers gone for ever.

In the midst of this crowd of beggars and shamefaced creatures some lordly carriage passed from time to time containing a Fox, or a thieving Magpie, or some ravenous bird of prey.

'And where is the Field of Miracles?' asked Pinocchio.

'It is here, not two steps from us.'

They crossed the town, and having gone beyond the walls they came to a solitary field which at first sight resembled all other fields.

'We are arrived,' said the Fox to the puppet. 'Now stoop down and dig with your hands a little hole in the ground and put your gold pieces into it.'

Pinocchio obeyed. He dug a hole, put into it the four gold pieces that he had left, and then filled up the hole with a little earth.

'Now then,' said the Fox, 'go to that canal close to us, fetch a can of water, and water the ground where you have sowed them.'

Pinocchio went to the canal, and as he had no can he took off one of his old shoes, and filling it with water he watered the ground over the hole.

He then asked:

'Is there anything else to be done?'

'Nothing else,' answered the Fox. 'We can now go away. You can return in about twenty minutes, and you will find a shrub already pushing through the ground, with its branches quite loaded with money.'

The poor puppet, beside himself with joy, thanked the Fox and the Cat a thousand times, and promised them a beautiful present.

'We wish for no presents,' answered the two rascals. 'It is enough for us to have taught you the way to enrich yourself without undergoing hard work, and we are as happy as folk out for a holiday.'

Thus saying they took leave of Pinocchio, and, wishing him a good harvest, went about their business.

XIX

PINOCCHIO IS ROBBED OF HIS MONEY, AND AS A PUNISHMENT HE IS SENT TO PRISON FOR FOUR MONTHS.

THE PUPPET RETURNED to the town and began to count the minutes one by one; and when he thought that it must be time he took the road leading to the Field of Miracles.

And as he walked along with hurried steps his heart beat fast, tic, tac, tic, tac, like a drawing-room clock when it is really going well. Meanwhile he was thinking to himself:

'And if instead of a thousand gold pieces I was to find on the branches of the tree two thousand? . . . And instead of two thousand supposing I found five thousand? and instead of five thousand that I found a hundred thousand? Oh! what a fine gentleman I should then become! . . . I would have a beautiful palace, a thousand little wooden horses and a thousand stables to amuse myself with, a cellar full of currant-wine and sweet syrups, and a library quite full of candies, tarts, plum-cakes, macaroons, and cream biscuits.'

Whilst he was building these castles in the air he had arrived in the neighbourhood of the field, and he stopped to look if by chance he could perceive a tree with its branches laden with money; but he saw nothing. He advanced another hundred steps—nothing: he entered the field . . . he went right up to the

'You ill-mannered Parrot'

little hole where he had buried his sovereigns—and nothing. He then became very thoughtful, and forgetting the rules of society and good manners he took his hands out of his pocket and gave his head a long scratch.

At that moment he heard an explosion of laughter close to him, and looking up he saw a large Parrot perched on a tree, who was pruning the few feathers he had left.

'Why are you laughing?' asked Pinocchio in an angry voice.

'I am laughing because in pruning my feathers I tickled myself under my wings.'

The puppet did not answer, but went to the canal and, filling the same old shoe full of water, he proceeded to water the earth afresh that covered his gold pieces.

Whilst he was thus occupied another laugh, and still more impertinent than the first, rang out in the silence of that solitary place.

'Once for all,' shouted Pinocchio in a rage, 'may I know, you ill-mannered Parrot, what you are laughing at?'

'I am laughing at those simpletons who believe in all the foolish things that are told them, and who allow themselves to be entrapped by those who are more cunning than they are.'

'Are you perhaps speaking of me?'

'Yes, I am speaking of you, poor Pinocchio—of you who are simple enough to believe that money can be sown and gathered in fields in the same way as beans and pumpkins. I also believed it once, and to-day I am suffering for it. To-day—but it is too late—I have at last learnt that to put a few pennies honestly together it is necessary to know how to earn them, either by the work of our own hands or by the cleverness of our own brains.'

'I don't understand you,' said the puppet, who was already trembling with fear.

'Have patience! I will explain myself better,' rejoined the Parrot. 'You must know, then, that whilst you were in the town the Fox and the Cat returned to the field: they took the buried money and then fled like the wind. And now he that catches them will be clever.'

Pinocchio remained with his mouth open, and not choosing to believe the Parrot's words he began with his hands and nails to dig up the earth that he had watered. And he dug, and dug, and dug, and made such a deep hole that a rick of straw might have stood upright in it: but the money was no longer there.

He rushed back to the town in a state of desperation, and went at once to the courts of justice to denounce the two knaves who had robbed him to the judge.

The judge was a big ape of the gorilla tribe—an old ape respectable for his age, his white beard, but especially for his gold spectacles without glasses that he was always obliged to wear, on account of an inflammation of the eyes that had tormented him for many years.

Pinocchio related in the presence of the judge all the particulars of the infamous fraud of which he had been the victim. He gave the names, the surnames, and other details, of the two rascals, and ended by demanding justice.

The judge listened with great benignity; took a lively interest in the story; was much touched and moved; and when the puppet had nothing further to say he stretched out his hand and rang a bell.

At this summons two mastiffs immediately appeared dressed as policemen. The judges then, pointing to Pinocchio, said to them:

'That poor devil has been robbed of four gold pieces; take him off and put him immediately into prison.'

The puppet was petrified on hearing this unexpected sentence, and tried to protest; but the policemen, to avoid losing time, stopped his mouth, and carried him off to the lock-up.

And there he remained for four months—four long months —and he would have remained longer still if a fortunate chance had not released him. For I must tell you that the young Emperor who reigned over Booby Town, having won a splendid victory over his enemies, ordered great public rejoicings. There were illuminations, fireworks, horse races, and bicycle races, and as a further sign of triumph he commanded that the prisons should be opened and all the prisoners set at liberty.

'If the others are to be let out of prison I will go also,' said Pinocchio to the jailer.

'No, not you,' said the jailer, 'because you do not belong to the fortunate class.'

'I beg your pardon,' replied Pinocchio, 'I am also a criminal.'

'In that case you are perfectly right,' said the jailer; and taking off his hat and bowing to him respectfully he opened the prison doors and let him escape.

XX

FREED FROM PRISON, HE STARTS TO RETURN TO THE FAIRY'S HOUSE; BUT ON THE ROAD HE MEETS WITH A HORRIBLE SERPENT, AND AFTERWARDS HE IS CAUGHT IN A TRAP.

YOU CAN IMAGINE Pinocchio's joy when he found himself free. Without stopping to take breath he immediately left the town and took the road that led to the Fairy's house.

On account of the rainy weather the road had become a marsh into which he sank knee-deep. But the puppet would not give in. Tormented by the desire of seeing his father and his little sister with blue hair again he ran and leapt like a greyhound, and as he ran he was splashed with mud from head to foot. And he said to himself as he went along: 'How many misfortunes have happened to me ... and I deserved them! for I am an obstinate, self-willed puppet. ... I am always bent upon having my own way, without listening to those who wish me well, and who have a thousand times more sense than I have! ... But from this time forth I am determined to change and to become orderly and obedient. ... For at last I have seen that disobedient boys come to no good and gain nothing. And will my papa have waited for me? Shall I find him at the Fairy's house! Poor man, it is so long since I last saw him: I am dying to embrace him, and to cover him with kisses! And will the Fairy forgive me my bad conduct to her? ... To think of all the kindness and loving care I received from her ... to think that if I am now alive I owe it to her! ...

The poor puppet had been caught in a trap

Would it be possible to find a more ungrateful boy, or one with
less heart than I have!'

   Whilst he was saying this he stopped suddenly, frightened to
death, and made four steps backwards.

   What had he seen?

   He had seen an immense Serpent stretched across the road.
Its skin was green, it had red eyes, and a pointed tail that was
smoking like a chimney.

It would be impossible to imagine the puppet's terror. He walked away to a safe distance, and sitting down on a heap of stones waited until the Serpent should have gone about its business and had left the road clear.

He waited an hour; two hours; three hours; but the Serpent was always there, and even from a distance he could see the red light of his fiery eyes and the column of smoke that ascended from the end of his tail.

At last Pinocchio, trying to feel courageous, approached to within a few steps, and said to the Serpent in a small, soft, insinuating voice:

'Excuse me, Mr. Serpent, but would you be so good as to move a little to one side, just enough to allow me to pass?'

He might as well have spoken to the wall. Nobody moved.

He began again in the same soft voice:

'You must know, Mr. Serpent, that I am on my way home, where my father is waiting for me, and it is such a long time since I saw him last! . . . Will you therefore allow me to continue my road?'

He waited for a sign in answer to this request, but there was none: in fact the Serpent, who up to that moment had been sprightly and full of life, became motionless and almost rigid. He shut his eyes and his tail ceased smoking.

'Can he really be dead?' said Pinocchio, rubbing his hands with delight; and he determined to jump over him and reach the other side of the road. But just as he was going to leap the Serpent raised himself suddenly on end, like a spring set in motion; and the puppet, drawing back, in his terror caught his foot and fell to the ground.

And he fell so awkwardly that his head stuck in the mud and his legs went into the air.

At the sight of the puppet kicking violently with his head in the mud the Serpent went into convulsions of laughter, and he laughed, and laughed, and laughed, until from the violence of his laughter he broke a blood-vessel in his chest and died. And that time he was really dead.

Pinocchio then set off running in hopes that he should reach the Fairy's house before dark. But before long he began to suffer so dreadfully from hunger that he could not bear it, and he jumped into a field by the wayside intending to pick some bunches of muscatel grapes. Oh, that he had never done it!

He had scarcely reached the vines when crac . . . his legs were caught between two sharp iron bars, and he became so giddy with pain that stars of every colour danced before his eyes.

The poor puppet had been caught in a trap put there to capture some big polecats who were the scourge of the poultry-yards in the neighbourhood.

XXI

PINOCCHIO IS TAKEN BY A PEASANT, WHO OBLIGES HIM TO TAKE THE PLACE OF HIS WATCH-DOG IN THE POULTRY-YARD.

PINOCCHIO, as you can imagine, began to cry and scream: but his tears and groans were useless, for there was not a house to be seen, and not a living soul passed down the road.

At last night came on.

Partly from the pain of the trap that cut his legs, and a little from fear at finding himself alone in the dark in the midst of the fields, the puppet was on the point of fainting. Just at that moment he saw a Firefly flitting over his head. He called to it and said:

'Oh, little Firefly, will you have pity on me and free me from this torture?'

'Poor boy!' said the Firefly, stopping and looking at him with compassion, 'but how could your legs have been caught by those sharp irons?'

'I came into the field to pick two bunches of these muscatel grapes, and——'

'But were the grapes yours?'

'No.'

'Then who taught you to carry off other people's property?'

'I was so hungry.'

'Hunger, my boy, is not a good reason for taking what does not belong to us.'

'That is true, that is true!' said Pinocchio, crying. 'I will never do it again.'

'You shall be my watch-dog'

At this moment their conversation was interrupted by the soft sound of approaching footsteps. It was the owner of the field coming on tiptoe to see if one of the polecats that ate his chickens during the night had been caught in his trap.

His astonishment was great when, having brought out his lantern from under his coat, he perceived that instead of a polecat it was a boy who had been caught.

'Ah, little thief!' said the angry peasant, 'then it's you who carry off my chickens?'

'No, it is not me; indeed it is not!' cried Pinocchio, sobbing. 'I only came into the field to take two bunches of grapes!'

'He who steals grapes is quite capable of stealing chickens. Leave it to me, I'll give you a lesson that you won't forget in a hurry.'

Opening the trap he seized the puppet by the collar, and carried him to his house as if he had been a young lamb.

When he reached the yard in front of the house he threw him roughly on the ground, and putting his foot on his neck he said to him:

'It is late, and I want to go to bed; we will settle our accounts to-morrow. In the meanwhile, as the dog who kept guard at night died to-day, you shall take his place at once. You shall be my watch-dog.'

And taking a great collar covered with brass knobs he strapped it tightly round his throat that he might not be able to draw his head out of it. A heavy chain attached to the collar was fastened to the wall.

'If it should rain to-night,' he then said to him, 'you can go and lie down in the kennel; the straw that has served as a bed for my poor dog for the last four years is still there. If unfortunately robbers should come, remember to listen sharply and to bark.'

After giving him this last injunction the man went into the house, shut the door, and put up the chain.

Poor Pinocchio remained lying on the ground more dead than alive from the effects of cold, hunger, and fear. From time to time he put his hands angrily to the collar that tightened his throat and said, crying:

'It serves me right! . . . Decidedly it serves me right! I was determined to be a vagabond and a good-for-nothing. . . . I would listen to bad companions, and that is why I always meet with misfortunes. If I had been a good little boy as so many are; if I had been willing to learn and to work; if I had remained at home with my poor papa, I should not now be in the midst of the fields and obliged to be the watch-dog to a peasant's house. Oh, if I could be born again! But now it is too late, and I must have patience!'

Relieved by this little outburst, which came straight from his heart, he went into the dog-kennel and fell asleep.

XXII

PINOCCHIO DISCOVERS THE ROBBERS, AND
AS A REWARD FOR HIS FIDELITY IS SET
AT LIBERTY.

HE HAD BEEN SLEEPING HEAVILY for about two hours when, towards midnight, he was roused by a whispering of strange voices that seemed to come from the courtyard. Putting the tip of his nose out of the kennel he saw four little beasts with dark fur, that looked like cats, standing consulting together. But they were not cats; they were polecats—carnivorous little animals, especially greedy for eggs and young chickens. One of the polecats, leaving his companions, came to the opening of the kennel and said in a low voice:

'Good evening, Melampo.'

'My name is not Melampo,' answered the puppet.

'Oh! then who are you?'

'I am Pinocchio.'

'And what are you doing here?'

'I am acting as watch-dog.'

'Then where is Melampo? Where is the old dog who lived in this kennel?'

'He died this morning.'

'Is he dead? Poor beast! He was so good. But judging you by your face I should say that you were also a good dog.'

'I beg your pardon, I am not a dog.'

'Not a dog? Then what are you?'

'I am a puppet.'

'And you are acting as watch-dog?'

'That is only too true—as a punishment.'

'Well, then, I will offer you the same conditions that we made with the late Melampo, and I am sure you will be satisfied with them.'

'What are these conditions?'

'One night a week you are to allow us to get into this poultry-yard as we have done hitherto, and to carry off eight chickens. Of these chickens seven are to be eaten by us, and one we will give to you, on the express understanding, however, that you pretend to be asleep, and that it never enters your head to bark and to wake the peasant.'

'Did Melampo act in this manner?' asked Pinocchio.

'Certainly, and we were always on the best terms with him. Sleep quietly, and rest assured that before we go we will leave by the kennel a beautiful chicken ready plucked for your breakfast to-morrow. Have we understood each other clearly?'

'Only too clearly!' answered Pinocchio, and he shook his head threateningly as much as to say: 'You shall hear of this shortly!'

The four polecats thinking themselves safe repaired to the poultry-yard, which was close to the kennel, and having opened the wooden gate with their teeth and claws, they slipped in one by one. But they had only just passed through when they heard the gate shut behind them with great violence.

It was Pinocchio who had shut it; and for greater security he put a large stone against it to keep it closed.

He then began to bark, and he barked exactly like a watch-dog: bow-wow, bow-wow.

Hearing the barking the peasant jumped out of bed, and taking his gun he came to the window and asked:

'What is the matter?'

'There are robbers!' answered Pinocchio.

'Where are they?'

'In the poultry-yard.'

'I will come down directly.'

In fact, in less time than it takes to say Amen the peasant came down. He rushed into the poultry-yard, caught the

The polecats . . . slipped in one by one

polecats, and having put them into a sack, he said to them in a
tone of great satisfaction:

'At last you have fallen into my hands! I might punish you,
but I am not so cruel. I will content myself instead by carrying
you in the morning to the innkeeper of the neighbouring village,
who will skin and cook you as hares with a sweet-sour sauce. It
is an honour that you don't deserve, but generous people like me
don't consider such trifles!'

He then approached Pinocchio and patted him, and amongst
other things he asked him:

'How did you manage to discover the four thieves? To think
that Melampo, my faithful Melampo, never found out anything!'

The puppet might then have told him the whole story; he
might have informed him of the disgraceful conditions that had
been made between the dog and the polecats; but he remembered
that the dog was dead, and he thought to himself:

'What is the good of accusing the dead? The dead are dead,
and the best thing to be done is to leave them in peace!'

'When the thieves got into the yard were you asleep or
awake?' the peasant went on to ask him.

'I was asleep,' answered Pinocchio, 'but the polecats woke
me with their chatter, and one of them came to the kennel and
said to me: "If you promise not to bark, and not to wake the
master, we will make you a present of a fine chicken ready
plucked!" To think that they should have had the audacity to
make such a proposal to me! For although I am a puppet, pos-

sessing perhaps nearly all the faults in the world, there is one that I certainly will never be guilty of, that of making terms with, and sharing in the gains of, dishonest people!'

'Well said, my boy!' cried the peasant, slapping him on the shoulder. 'Such sentiments do you honour: and as a proof of my gratitude I will at once set you at liberty, and you may return home.'

And he removed the dog's collar.

XXIII

PINOCCHIO MOURNS THE DEATH OF THE
BEAUTIFUL LITTLE GIRL WITH THE BLUE
HAIR. HE THEN MEETS WITH A PIGEON
WHO FLIES WITH HIM TO THE SEASHORE,
AND THERE HE THROWS HIMSELF INTO THE
WATER TO GO TO THE ASSISTANCE OF HIS
FATHER GEPPETTO.

AS SOON AS PINOCCHIO was released from the heavy and
humiliating weight of the dog-collar he started off across the
fields, and never stopped until he had reached the high road that
led to the Fairy's house. There he turned and looked down into
the plain beneath. He could see distinctly with his naked eye the
wood where he had been so unfortunate as to meet with the Fox
and the Cat; he could see amongst the trees the top of the Big
Oak to which he had been hung; but although he looked in every
direction the little house belonging to the beautiful Little Girl
with the blue hair was nowhere visible.

Seized with a sad presentiment he began to run with all the
strength he had left, and in a few minutes he reached the field
where the little white house had once stood. But the little white
house was no longer there. He saw instead a marble stone, on
which were engraved these sad words:

HERE LIES
THE LITTLE GIRL WITH THE BLUE HAIR
WHO DIED FROM SORROW
BECAUSE SHE WAS ABANDONED BY HER
LITTLE BROTHER PINOCCHIO

I leave you to imagine the puppet's feelings when he had with difficulty spelt out this epitaph. He fell with his face on the ground and, covering the tombstone with a thousand kisses, burst into an agony of tears. He cried all night, and when morning came he was still crying although he had no tears left, and his sobs and lamentations were so shrill and heart-breaking that they roused the echoes in the surrounding hills.

And as he wept he said:

'Oh, little Fairy, why did you die? Why did not I die instead of you, I who am so wicked, whilst you were so good? . . . And my papa? Where can he be? Oh, little Fairy, tell me where I can find him, for I want to remain with him always and never to leave him again, never again! . . . Oh, little Fairy, tell me that it is not true that you are dead! . . . If you really love me . . . if you really love your little brother, come to life again . . . come to life as you were before! . . . Does it not grieve you to see me alone and abandoned by everybody? . . . If assassins come they will hang me again to the branch of a tree . . . and then I should die indeed. What do you imagine that I can do here alone in the world? Now that I have lost you and my papa, who will give me food? Where shall I go to sleep at night? Who will make me a new jacket? Oh, it would be better, a hundred times better, that I should die also! Yes, I want to die . . . oh! oh! oh!'

And in his despair he tried to tear his hair; but his hair being made of wood, he could not even have the satisfaction of sticking his fingers into it.

Just then a large Pigeon flew over his head, and stopping with outspread wings called down to him from a great height:

'Tell me, child, what are you doing there?'

'Don't you see? I am crying!' said Pinocchio, raising his head towards the voice and rubbing his eyes with his jacket.

'Tell me,' continued the Pigeon, 'amongst your companions, do you happen to know a puppet who is called Pinocchio?'

'Pinocchio? . . . Did you say Pinocchio?' repeated the puppet, jumping quickly to his feet. 'I am Pinocchio!'

The Pigeon at this answer descended rapidly to the ground. He was larger than a turkey.

'Do you also know Geppetto?' he asked.

'Do I know him! He is my poor papa! Has he perhaps spoken to you of me? Will you take me to him? Is he still alive? Answer me for pity's sake: is he still alive?'

'I left him three days ago on the seashore.'

'What was he doing?'

'He was building a little boat for himself, to cross the ocean. For more than three months that poor man has been going all round the world looking for you. Not having succeeded in finding you he has now taken it into his head to go to the distant countries of the New World in search of you.'

'How far is it from here to the shore?' asked Pinocchio breathlessly.

'More than six hundred miles.'

'Six hundred miles? Oh, beautiful Pigeon, what a fine thing it would be to have your wings!'

'If you wish to go I will carry you there.'

'How?'

'Astride on my back. Do you weigh much?'

'I weigh next to nothing. I am as light as a feather.'

And without waiting for more Pinocchio jumped at once on the Pigeon's back, and putting a leg on each side of him, as men do on horseback, he exclaimed joyfully:

'Gallop, gallop, my little horse, for I am anxious to arrive quickly!'

The Pigeon took flight, and in a few minutes had soared so high that they almost touched the clouds. Finding himself at such an immense height the puppet had the curiosity to turn and look down; but his head spun round, and he became so frightened that to save himself from the danger of falling he wound his arms tightly round the neck of his feathered steed.

They flew all day. Towards evening the Pigeon said:

'I am very thirsty!'

'And I am very hungry!' rejoined Pinocchio.

'Let us stop at that dovecote for a few minutes; and then we will continue our journey so as to reach the seashore by dawn to-morrow.'

They went into a deserted dovecote, where they found nothing but a basin full of water and a basket full of lettuce.

The puppet had never in his life been able to eat lettuce: according to him it made him sick and revolted him. That evening, however, he ate his fill, and when he had nearly emptied the basket he turned to the Pigeon and said to him:

'I never could have believed that lettuce was so good!'

'You 'd better know, my boy,' replied the Pigeon, 'that when hunger is real, and there is nothing else to eat, even lettuce becomes delicious. Hunger knows nothing of whims or greed!'

Having quickly finished their little meal they recommenced their journey and flew away. The following morning they reached the seashore.

The Pigeon placed Pinocchio on the ground, and not wishing to be troubled with thanks for having done a good action, flew quickly away and disappeared.

The shore was crowded with people who were looking out to sea, shouting and gesticulating.

'What has happened?' asked Pinocchio of an old woman.

'A poor father who has lost his son has gone away in a boat to search for him on the other side of the water, and to-day the sea is tempestuous and the little boat is in danger of sinking.'

'Where is the little boat?'

'It is out there in a line with my finger,' said the old woman, pointing to a little boat which, seen at that distance, looked like a nutshell with a very little man in it.

Pinocchio fixed his eyes on it, and after looking attentively he gave a piercing scream, crying:

'It is my papa! it is my papa!'

The boat meanwhile, beaten by the fury of the waves, at one moment disappeared in the trough of the sea, and the next came again to the surface. Pinocchio, standing on the top of a high rock, kept calling to his father by name, and making every kind of signal to him with his hands, his handkerchief, and his cap.

And although he was so far off, Geppetto appeared to recognize his son, for he also took off his cap and waved it, and tried by gestures to make him understand that he would have returned

Pinocchio, standing on . . . a high rock, kept calling to his father

if it had been possible, but that the sea was so tempestuous that he could not use his oars or approach the shore.

Suddenly a tremendous wave rose and the boat disappeared. They waited, hoping it would come again to the surface, but it was seen no more.

'Poor man!' said the fishermen who were assembled on the shore, and murmuring a prayer they turned to go home.

Just then they heard a desperate cry, and looking back they saw a little boy who exclaimed, as he jumped from a rock into the sea:

'I will save my papa!'

Pinocchio, being made of wood, floated easily and he swam like a fish. At one moment they saw him disappear under the water, carried down by the fury of the waves; and next he reappeared struggling with a leg or an arm. At last they lost sight of him, and he was seen no more.

'Poor boy!' said the fishermen who were collected on the shore, and murmuring a prayer they returned home.

XXIV

PINOCCHIO ARRIVES AT THE ISLAND
OF THE BUSY BEES, AND FINDS
THE FAIRY AGAIN.

PINOCCHIO, hoping to be in time to help his father, swam the whole night.

And what a horrible night it was! The rain came down in torrents, it hailed, the thunder was frightful, and the flashes of lightning made it as light as day.

Towards morning he saw a long strip of land not far off. It was an island in the midst of the sea.

He tried his utmost to reach the shore: but it was all in vain. The waves, racing and tumbling over each other, knocked him about as if he had been a stick or a wisp of straw. At last, fortunately for him, a billow rolled up with such fury and impetuosity that he was lifted up and thrown violently far on to the sands.

He fell with such force that, as he struck the ground, his ribs and all his joints cracked, but he comforted himself, saying:

'I 've had another wonderful escape!'

Little by little the sky cleared, the sun shone out in all his splendour, and the sea became as quiet and smooth as oil.

The puppet put his clothes in the sun to dry, and began to look in every direction in hopes of seeing on the vast expanse of water a little boat with a little man in it. But although he looked and looked, he could see nothing but the sky, and the sea, and the sail of some ship, but so far away that it seemed no bigger than a fly.

'If I only knew what this island was called!' he said to himself. 'If I only knew whether it was inhabited by civilized people—I mean by people who have not got the bad habit of hanging boys to the branches of the trees. But who can I ask? who, if there is nobody?'

This idea of finding himself alone, alone, all alone, in the midst of this great uninhabited country, made him so melancholy that he was just beginning to cry. But at that moment, at a short distance from the shore, he saw a big fish swimming by; it was going quietly on its own business with its head out of the water.

Not knowing its name the puppet called to it in a loud voice to make himself heard:

'Hey, Mr. Fish, will you permit me a word with you?'

'Two if you like,' answered the fish, who was a Dolphin, and so polite that there were few like him in any sea in the world.

'Will you be kind enough to tell me if there are villages in this island where it would be possible to obtain something to eat, without running the danger of being eaten?'

'Certainly there are,' replied the Dolphin. 'Indeed you will find one at a short distance from here.'

'And what road must I take to go there?'

'You must take that path to your left and follow your nose. You cannot make a mistake.'

'Will you tell me another thing? You who swim about the sea all day and all night, have you by chance met a little boat with my papa in it?'

'And who is your papa?'

'He is the best papa in the world, whilst it would be difficult to find a worse son than I am.'

'During the terrible storm last night,' answered the Dolphin, 'the little boat must have gone to the bottom.'

'And my papa?'

'He must have been swallowed by the terrible Shark who for some days past has been spreading devastation and ruin in our waters.'

'Is this Shark very big?' asked Pinocchio, who was already beginning to quake with fear.

'Big!' replied the Dolphin. 'To give you some idea of his size I need only tell you that he is bigger than a five-storeyed house, and that his mouth is so enormous and so deep that a railway train with its smoking engine could pass easily down his throat.'

'Mercy upon us!' exclaimed the terrified puppet; and putting on his clothes with the greatest haste he said to the Dolphin:

'Good-bye, Mr. Fish: forgive me for the trouble I have given you, and many thanks for your politeness.'

He then took the path that had been pointed out to him and began to walk fast—so fast, indeed, that he was almost running. And at the slightest noise he turned to look behind him, fearing that he might see the terrible Shark with a railway train in its mouth following him.

After a walk of half an hour he reached a little village called the village of the Busy Bees. The road was alive with people running here and there minding their own business: all were at work, all had something to do. You could not have found an idler or a tramp, not even if you had searched for him with a lighted lamp.

'Ah!' said that lazy Pinocchio at once, 'I see that this village will never suit me! I wasn't born to work!'

In the meanwhile he was tormented by hunger, for he had eaten nothing for twenty-four hours—not even lettuce. What was he to do?

There were only two ways by which he could obtain food— either by asking for a little work, or by begging for a halfpenny or for a mouthful of bread.

He was ashamed to beg, for his father had always preached to him that no one had a right to beg except the aged and the infirm. The really poor in this world, deserving of compassion and assistance, are only those who from age or sickness are no longer able to earn their own bread with the labour of their hands. It is the duty of every one else to work; and if they will not work so much the worse for them if they suffer from hunger.

At that moment a man came down the road, tired and panting for breath. With pain and difficulty he was dragging along two carts full of charcoal.

Pinocchio, judging by his face that he was a kind man, approached him, and casting down his eyes with shame he said to him in a low voice:

'Would you have the charity to give me a half-penny, for I am dying of hunger?'

'You shall have not only a halfpenny,' said the man, 'but I will give you twopence, provided that you help me to drag home these two carts of charcoal.'

'I am surprised at you!' answered the puppet in an offended tone. 'Let me tell you that I am not accustomed to do the work of a donkey: I have never drawn a cart!'

'So much the better for you,' answered the man. 'Then, my boy, if you are really dying of hunger, eat two fine slices of your pride, and be careful not to get indigestion.'

A few minutes afterwards a mason passed down the road carrying on his shoulders a basket of lime.

'Would you have the charity, good man, to give a halfpenny to a poor boy who is yawning for want of food?'

'Willingly,' answered the man. 'Come with me and carry the lime, and instead of a halfpenny I will give you five.'

'But the lime is heavy,' objected Pinocchio, 'and I don't want to tire myself.'

'If you don't want to tire yourself, then, my boy, amuse yourself by yawning, and much good may it do you.'

In less than half an hour twenty other people went by; and Pinocchio asked charity of them all, but they all answered:

'Are you not ashamed to beg? Instead of idling about the roads, go and look for a little work and learn to earn your bread.'

At last a nice little woman carrying two cans of water came by.

'Will you let me drink a little water out of your can?' asked Pinocchio, who was burning with thirst.

'Drink, my boy, if you wish it!' said the little woman, setting down the two cans.

Pinocchio drank like a fish, and as he dried his mouth he mumbled:

'I have quenched my thirst. If I could only satisfy my hunger! . . .'

The good woman hearing these words said at once:

'If you will help me to carry home these two cans of water I will give you a fine piece of bread.'

Pinocchio looked at the cans and answered neither yes nor no.

'Amuse yourself by yawning, and much good may it do you'

'And besides the bread you shall have a nice dish of cauliflower dressed with oil and vinegar,' added the good woman.

Pinocchio gave another look at the cans, and answered neither yes nor no.

'And after the cauliflower I will give you a beautiful sweetmeat full of syrup.'

The temptation of this last dainty was so great that Pinocchio could resist no longer, and with an air of decision he said:

'I must have patience! I will carry one of the cans to your house.'

The can was heavy, and the puppet, not being strong enough to carry it in his hand, had to resign himself to carrying it on his head.

When they reached the house the good little woman made Pinocchio sit down at a small table already laid, and she placed before him the bread, the cauliflower, and the sweetmeat.

Pinocchio did not eat, he devoured. His stomach was like a room that had been left empty and uninhabited for five months.

When his ravenous hunger was somewhat appeased he raised his head to thank his benefactress; but he had no sooner looked at her than he gave a prolonged Oh-h-h! of astonishment, and continued staring at her, with wide-open eyes, his fork in the air, and his mouth full of bread and cauliflower, as if he had been be-witched.

'What has surprised you so much?' asked the good woman, laughing.

'It is . . .' answered the puppet, 'it is . . . it is . . . that you are like . . . that you remind me . . . yes, yes, yes, the same voice . . . the same eyes . . . the same hair . . . yes, yes, yes . . . you also have blue hair . . . as she had. . . . Oh, little Fairy! . . . tell me that it is you, really you! . . . Do not make me cry any more! If you knew . . . I have cried so much, I have suffered so much.'

And throwing himself at her feet on the floor Pinocchio embraced the knees of the mysterious little woman and began to cry bitterly.

XXV

PINOCCHIO PROMISES THE FAIRY TO BE
GOOD AND STUDIOUS, FOR HE IS QUITE
SICK OF BEING A PUPPET AND WISHES TO
BECOME AN EXEMPLARY BOY.

AT FIRST the good little woman maintained that she was not the little Fairy with blue hair; but seeing that she was found out, and not wishing to continue the comedy any longer, she ended by making herself known, and she said to Pinocchio:

'You little rogue! how did you ever discover who I was?'

'It was my great affection for you that told me.'

'Do you remember? You left me a child, and now that you have found me again I am a woman—a woman almost old enough to be your mamma.'

'I am delighted at that, for now, instead of calling you little sister I will call you mamma. I have wished for such a long time to have a mamma like other boys! . . . But how did you manage to grow so fast?'

'That is a secret.'

'Teach it to me, for I should also like to grow. Don't you see? I always remain no bigger than a ha'p'orth of cheese!'

'But you cannot grow,' replied the Fairy.

'Why?'

'Because puppets never grow. They are born puppets, live puppets, and die puppets.'

'Oh, I'm sick of being a puppet!' cried Pinocchio, giving himself a slap. 'It is time that I became a man.'

'And you will become one if you know how to deserve it.'

'Not really? And what can I do to deserve it?'

'A very easy thing: by learning to be a good boy.'

'And you think I am not?'

'You are quite the contrary. Good boys are obedient, and you——'

'And I never obey.'

'Good boys like to learn and to work, and you——'

'And I instead lead an idle vagabond life the whole year through.'

'Good boys always speak the truth——'

'And I always tell lies.'

'Good boys go willingly to school——'

'And school gives me pain all over my body. But from to-day I will change my life.'

'Do you promise me?'

'I promise you. I will become a good little boy, and I will be a comfort to my papa. . . . Where is my poor papa at this moment?'

'I do not know.'

'Shall I ever have the happiness of seeing him again and kissing him?'

'I think so; indeed I am sure of it.'

At this answer Pinocchio was so delighted that he took the Fairy's hands and began to kiss them with such fervour that he seemed beside himself. Then raising his face and looking at her lovingly he asked:

'Tell me, little mamma: then it was not true that you were dead?'

'It seems not,' said the Fairy, smiling.

'If you only knew the sorrow I felt and the tightening of my throat when I read "Here lies . . ." '

'I know it, and it is on that account that I have forgiven you. I saw from the sincerity of your grief that you had a good heart; and when boys have good hearts, even if they are scamps and have got bad habits, there is always something to hope for: that is, there is always hope that they will turn to better ways. That is why I came to look for you here. I will be your mamma.'

'Oh, how delightful!' shouted Pinocchio, jumping for joy.

'You must obey me and do everything that I bid you.'

'Willingly, willingly, willingly!'

'To-morrow,' rejoined the Fairy, 'you will begin to go to school.'

Pinocchio became at once a little less joyful.

'Then you must choose an art, or a trade, according to your own wishes.'

Pinocchio became very grave.

'What are you muttering between your teeth?' asked the Fairy in an angry voice.

'I was saying,' moaned the puppet in a low voice, 'that it seemed to me too late for me to go to school now.'

'No, sir. Keep it in mind that it is never too late to learn and to acquire knowledge.'

'But I do not wish to follow either an art or a trade.'

'Why?'

'Because it tires me to work.'

'My boy,' said the Fairy, 'those who talk in that way end almost always either in prison or in the hospital. Let me tell you that every man, whether he is born rich or poor, is obliged to do something in this world—to occupy his time, to work. Woe to those who lead slothful lives. Sloth is a dreadful illness and must be cured at once, in childhood. If not, when we are old it can never be cured.'

Pinocchio was touched by these words, and lifting his head quickly he said to the Fairy:

'I will study, I will work, I will do all that you tell me, for indeed I have become weary of being a puppet, and I wish at any price to become a boy. You promised me that I should, didn't you?'

'I did promise you, and it now depends upon yourself.'

XXVI

PINOCCHIO ACCOMPANIES HIS
SCHOOLFELLOWS TO THE SEASHORE TO SEE
THE TERRIBLE SHARK.

THE FOLLOWING DAY Pinocchio went to the elementary school.

Imagine the delight of all the little rogues when they saw a puppet walk into their school! They set up a roar of laughter that never ended. They played him all sorts of tricks. One boy carried off his cap, another pulled his jacket behind; one tried to give him a pair of inky mustachios just under his nose, and another attempted to tie strings to his feet and hands to make him dance.

For a short time Pinocchio pretended not to care and got on as well as he could; but at last, losing all patience, he turned to those who were teasing him most and making fun of him, and said to them, looking very angry:

'Look out, boys: I am not here to be your buffoon. I respect others, and I intend to be respected.'

'Well said, gas-bag! You talk like a book!' howled the young rascals, doubled up with loud laughter; and one of them, more impudent than the others, stretched out his hand intending to seize the puppet by the end of his nose.

But he was not in time, for Pinocchio stuck his leg out from under the table and gave him a great kick on his shins.

'Oh, what hard feet!' roared the boy, rubbing the bruise that the puppet had given him.

'And what elbows! . . . even harder than his feet!' said an-

They played him all sorts of tricks

other, who for his rude tricks had received a blow in the region of his tummy.

But nevertheless the kick and the blow acquired at once for Pinocchio the sympathy and the esteem of all the boys in the school. They all made friends with him and liked him heartily.

And even the teacher praised him, for he found him attentive, studious, and intelligent—always the first to come to school, and the last to leave when school was over.

But he had one fault: he made too many friends; and amongst them were several young rascals well known for their dislike to study and love of mischief.

The teacher warned him every day, and even the good Fairy never failed to tell him, and to repeat constantly:

'Take care, Pinocchio! Those bad schoolfellows of yours will end sooner or later by making you lose all love of study, and perhaps even they may bring upon you some great misfortune.'

'There is no fear of that!' answered the puppet, shrugging his shoulders, and touching his forehead as much as to say: 'There is so much sense here!'

Now it happened that one fine day as he was on his way to school he met several of his usual companions who, coming up to him, asked:

'Have you heard the great news?'

'No.'

'In the sea near here a Shark has appeared as big as a mountain.'

'Not really? Can it be the same Shark that was there when

my poor papa was drowned?'

'We are going to the shore to see him. Will you come with us?'

'No; I am going to school.'

'Don't bother about school. We can go to school to-morrow. Whether we have a lesson more or a lesson less, we shall always be the same blockheads.'

'But what will the teacher say?'

'The teacher may say what he likes. He is paid on purpose to grumble all day.'

'And my mamma?'

'Mammas know nothing,' answered those bad little boys.

'Do you know what I will do?' said Pinocchio. 'I have reasons for wishing to see the Shark, but I will go and see him when school is over.'

'You poor idiot!' exclaimed one of the number. 'Do you suppose that a fish of that size will wait your convenience? As soon as he is tired of being here he will go on to another place, and then it will be too late.'

'How long does it take from here to the shore?' asked the puppet.

'We can be there and back in an hour.'

'Then away!' shouted Pinocchio, 'and he who runs fastest is the best!'

Having thus been given the signal to start, the boys, with their books and copy-books under their arms, rushed off across the fields, and Pinocchio was always the first—he seemed to have wings to his feet.

From time to time he turned to jeer at his companions, who were some distance behind, and seeing them panting for breath, covered with dust and their tongues hanging out of their mouths, he laughed heartily. The unfortunate boy little knew the terrors and terrible disasters that lay ahead of him.

XXVII

A GREAT FIGHT BETWEEN PINOCCHIO AND
HIS COMPANIONS. ONE OF THEM IS
WOUNDED, AND PINOCCHIO IS ARRESTED
BY THE POLICE.

WHEN HE ARRIVED on the shore Pinocchio looked out to sea;
for he saw no Shark. The sea was as smooth as a great crystal
mirror.

'Where is the Shark?' he asked, turning to his companions.

'He must have gone to his breakfast,' said one of them,
laughing.

'Or he has thrown himself on to his bed to have a little nap,'
added another, laughing still louder.

From their absurd answers and silly laughter Pinocchio perceived that his schoolfellows had been making a fool of him, in
inducing him to believe a tale with no truth in it. He was very
much put out, and he said to them angrily:

'And now? May I ask what fun you've found in deceiving
me with the story of the Shark?'

'Oh, it was great fun!' answered the little rascals in chorus.

'And in what did it consist?'

'In making you miss school, and persuading you to come
with us. Aren't you ashamed of being always so punctual and so

diligent with your lessons? Aren't you ashamed of studying so hard?'

'Suppose I do? It 's no business of yours.'

'It certainly is, because it puts us in a bad light with the teacher.'

'Why?'

'Because boys who work at their lessons make those who don't wish to learn anything seem worse. That's just too bad. We have our pride, you know.'

'Then what do you want me to do?'

'You must do the same as we do and hate school, lessons, and the teacher—our three greatest enemies.'

'Suppose I want to go on studying?'

'In that case we'll have nothing more to do with you, and we'll take the first chance of making you pay for it.'

'Really,' said the puppet, shaking his head. 'You make me want to laugh.'

'Now, Pinocchio,' shouted the biggest of the boys, confronting him. 'None of your superior airs: don't come here to crow over us! . . . for if you are not afraid of us, we are not afraid of you. Remember that you are one against seven of us.'

'Seven, like the seven deadly sins,' said Pinocchio with a shout of laughter.

'Listen to him! He has insulted us all! He called us the seven deadly sins!'

'Pinocchio! beg pardon . . . or it will be the worse for you!'

'Cuckoo!' sang the puppet, putting his forefinger to the end of his nose scoffingly.

'Pinocchio! it will end badly!'

'Cuckoo!'

'You will get as many blows as a donkey!'

'Cuckoo!'

'You will return home with a broken nose!'

'Cuckoo!'

'Ah, you shall have the cuckoo from me!' said the most courageous of the boys. 'Take that to begin with, and keep it for your supper to-night.'

And so saying he gave him a blow on the head with his fist.

But it was give and take; for the puppet, as was to be expected, immediately returned the blow, and the fight in a moment became general and desperate.

Pinocchio, although he was one alone, defended himself like a hero. He used his feet, which were of the hardest wood, to such purpose that he kept his enemies at a respectful distance. Wherever they touched they left a bruise by way of reminder.

The boys, becoming furious at not being able to measure themselves hand to hand with the puppet, had recourse to other weapons. Loosening their satchels they commenced throwing their school-books at him—grammars, dictionaries, spelling-books, geography books, and any other books they happened to have. But Pinocchio was quick and had sharp eyes, and always managed to duck in time, so that the books passed over his head and all fell into the sea.

Just think of the astonishment of the fishes! Thinking that the books were something to eat they all arrived in shoals, but having tasted a page or two, or a frontispiece, they spat it quickly out and made a wry face that seemed to say: 'It isn't food for us; we are accustomed to something much better!'

Gave him a blow on the head with his fist

The battle meantime had become fiercer than ever, when a big crab, who had come out of the water and had climbed slowly

up on to the shore, called out in a hoarse voice that sounded like
a trumpet with a bad cold:

'Have done with that, you young ruffians, for you are nothing else! These hand-to-hand fights between boys seldom finish
well. Some disaster is sure to happen!'

Poor crab! He might as well have preached to the wind.
Even that young rascal Pinocchio, turning round, looked at him
mockingly and said rudely:

'Hold your tongue, you silly old crab! You had better suck
some liquorice lozenges to cure that cold in your throat. Or better still, go to bed and sweat it out of you!'

Just then the boys, who had no more books of their own to
throw, spied at a little distance the satchel that belonged to
Pinocchio, and took possession of it in less than it takes to tell.

Amongst the books there was one bound in strong cardboard with the back and corners of parchment. It was a treatise
on arithmetic. I leave you to judge if it was big or not!

One of the boys seized this volume, and aiming at Pinocchio's head threw it at him with all the force he could muster. But
instead of hitting the puppet it struck one of his companions on
the temple, who, turning as white as a sheet, said only:

'Oh, mother, help . . . I am dying! . . .' and measured his
length on the sand. Thinking he was dead the terrified boys ran
off as hard as their legs could carry them, and in a few minutes
they were out of sight.

But Pinocchio remained. Although from grief and fright he
was more dead than alive, nevertheless he ran and soaked his
handkerchief in the sea and began to bathe the temples of his
poor schoolfellow. Crying bitterly in his despair he kept calling
him by name and saying to him:

'Eugene! . . . my poor Eugene! . . . open your eyes and look
at me! . . . why do you not answer? I did not do it, indeed it was
not I that hurt you so! believe me, it was not! Open your eyes,
Eugene. . . . If you keep your eyes shut I shall die too. . . . Oh!
what shall I do? how shall I ever return home? How can I ever
have the courage to go back to my good mamma? What will become of me? . . . Where can I fly to? . . . Oh! how much better it
would have been, a thousand times better, if I had only gone to

school! . . . Why did I listen to my schoolfellows? they have been my ruin. The master said to me, and my mamma repeated it often: 'Beware of bad companions!' But I am obstinate . . a wilful fool. . . . I let them talk and then I always take my own way! and I have to suffer for it. . . . And so, ever since I have been in the world, I have never had a happy quarter of an hour. Oh dear! what will become of me, what will become of me, what will become of me?'

And Pinocchio began to cry and sob, and to strike his head with his fists, and to call poor Eugene by his name. Suddenly he heard the sound of approaching footsteps.

He turned and saw two policemen.

'What are you doing there lying on the ground?' they asked Pinocchio.

'I am helping my schoolfellow.'

'Has he been hurt?'

'So it seems.'

'Hurt indeed!' said one of the policemen, stooping down and examining Eugene closely. 'This boy has been wounded in the temple. Who wounded him?'

'Not I,' stammered the puppet breathlessly.

'If it was not you, who then did it?'

'Not I,' repeated Pinocchio.

'And with what was he wounded?'

'With this book.' And the puppet picked up from the ground the treatise on arithmetic, bound in cardboard and parchment, and showed it to the policemen.

'And to whom does this book belong?'

'To me.'

'That is enough: nothing more is wanted. Get up and come with us at once.'

'But I——'

'Come along with us!'

'But I am innocent.'

'Come along with us!'

Before they left the policemen called some fishermen who were passing at that moment near the shore in their boat, and said to them:

'We give this boy who has been wounded in the head into your charge. Carry him to your house and nurse him. To-morrow we will come and see him.'

They then turned to Pinocchio, and having placed him between them they said to him in a commanding voice:

'Forward! and walk quickly! or it will be the worse for you.'

Without requiring it to be repeated the puppet set out along the road leading to the village. But the poor little wretch hardly knew where he was. He thought he must be dreaming, and what a dreadful dream! He was beside himself. He saw double: his legs shook: his tongue clung to the roof of his mouth, and he could not utter a word. And yet in the midst of his stupefaction and apathy his heart was pierced by a cruel thorn—the thought that he would have to pass under the windows of the good Fairy's house walking between two policemen. He would rather have died.

They had already reached the village when a gust of wind blew Pinocchio's cap off his head and carried it ten yards off.

'Will you give me leave,' said the puppet to the policemen, 'to go and get my cap?'

'Go, then; but be quick about it.'

The puppet went and picked up his cap . . . but instead of putting it on his head he took it between his teeth and began to run as hard as he could towards the seashore.

The policemen, thinking it would be difficult to overtake him, sent after him a large mastiff who had won the first prizes at all the dog-races. Pinocchio ran, but the dog ran faster. The people came to their windows and crowded into the street in their anxiety to see the end of the desperate race. But they could not satisfy their curiosity, for Pinocchio and the dog raised such clouds of dust that in a few minutes nothing could be seen of either of them.

XXVIII

PINOCCHIO IS IN DANGER OF BEING FRIED
IN A FRYING-PAN LIKE A FISH.

THERE CAME A MOMENT in this desperate race—a terrible moment when Pinocchio thought himself lost: for you must know that Alidoro—for so the mastiff was called—had run so swiftly that he had nearly come up with him.

The puppet could hear the panting of the dreadful beast close behind him; there was not a hand's breadth between them, he could even feel the dog's hot breath.

Fortunately the shore was close and the sea but a few steps off.

As soon as he reached the sands the puppet made a wonderful leap—a frog could have done no better—and plunged into the water.

Alidoro, on the contrary, wished to stop himself; but carried away by the impetus of the race he also fell into the sea. The unfortunate dog could not swim, but he made great efforts to keep himself afloat with his paws; but the more he struggled the farther he sank head downwards under the water.

When he rose to the surface again his eyes were rolling with terror, and he barked out:

'I am drowning! I am drowning!'

'Drown!' shouted Pinocchio from a distance, seeing himself safe from all danger.

'Help me, dear Pinocchio! . . . save me from death!'

At that agonizing cry the puppet, who had in reality an excellent heart, was moved with compassion, and turning to the dog he said:

'But if I save your life will you promise to give me no further annoyance, and not to run after me?'

'I promise! I promise! Be quick, for pity's sake, for if you delay another half-minute I shall be dead.'

Pinocchio hesitated: but remembering that his father had often told him that a good action is never lost, he swam to Alidoro, and taking hold of his tail with both hands brought him safe and sound on to the dry sand of the beach.

The poor dog could not stand. He had swallowed, against his will, so much salt water that he was like a balloon. The puppet, however, not wishing to trust him too far, thought it more prudent to jump again into the water. When he had swum some distance from the shore he called out to the friend he had rescued:

'Good-bye, Alidoro; a good journey to you, and my regards to all at home.'

'Good-bye, Pinocchio,' answered the dog; 'a thousand thanks for having saved my life. You have done me a great service, and in this world you get back what you give. If a chance comes along I shan't forget it.'

Pinocchio swam on, keeping always near the land. At last he thought that he had reached a safe place. Giving a look along the shore he saw amongst the rocks a kind of cave from which a cloud of smoke was ascending.

'In that cave,' he said to himself, 'there must be a fire. So much the better. I will go and dry and warm myself, and then? . . . and then we shall see.'

Having taken this resolution he approached the rocks; but as he was going to climb up he felt something under the water that rose higher and higher and carried him into the air. He tried to escape, but it was too late, for to his extreme surprise he found himself enclosed in a great net, together with a swarm of fish of every size and shape, who were flapping and struggling like so many souls in torment.

At the same moment a fisherman came out of the cave; he was so ugly, so horribly ugly, that he looked like a sea monster. Instead of hair his head was covered with a thick bush of green grass, his skin was green, his eyes were green, his long beard that

came down to the ground was also green. He had the appearance
of an immense lizard standing up on end.

When the fisherman had drawn his net out of the sea he exclaimed with great satisfaction:

'Thank Heaven! Once more I shall have a splendid feast of
fish to-day!'

'What a mercy that I am not a fish!' said Pinocchio to himself, regaining a little courage.

The net full of fish was carried into the cave, which was dark
and smoky. In the middle of the cave a large frying pan full of oil
was frying, and sending out a smell of mushrooms that was suf-
focating.

'Now we will see what fish we have taken!' said the green
fisherman; and putting into the net an enormous hand, so out of
all proportion that it looked like a baker's shovel, he pulled out a
handful of mullet.

'These mullet are good!' he said, looking at them and
smelling them complacently. And after he had smelt them he
threw them into a pan without water.

He repeated the same operation many times; and as he drew
out the fish his mouth watered and he said, chuckling to himself:

'What good whiting!'

'What exquisite sardines!'

'These soles are delicious!'

'This bass is choice indeed!'

'What dear little anchovies!'

I need not tell you that the whiting, the sardines, the soles,
the bass, and the anchovies were all thrown pellmell into the pan
to keep company with the mullet.

The last to remain in the net was Pinocchio.

No sooner had the fisherman taken him out than he opened
his big green eyes with astonishment, and cried, half frightened:

'What kind of fish is this? I never remember having eaten a
fish like this!'

And he looked at him again attentively, and having examined
him well all over he ended by saying:

'I know: he must be a crab.'

Pinocchio, mortified at being mistaken for a crab, said in an
angry voice:

'What kind of fish is this?'

'A crab indeed! do you take me for a crab? What treatment! Let me tell you that I am a puppet.'

'A puppet?' replied the fisherman. 'To tell the truth a puppet is quite a new fish for me. All the better! I shall eat you with greater pleasure.'

'Eat me! but will you understand that I am not a fish? Don't you hear that I talk as sensibly as you do?'

'That is quite true, said the fisherman; 'and as I see that you are a fish possessed of the talent of talking and reasoning as I do I will treat you with all the attention that is your due.'

'And this attention?'

'In token of my friendship and particular regard I will leave you the choice of how you would like to be cooked. Would you like to be fried in the frying-pan, or would you prefer to be stewed with tomato sauce?'

'To tell the truth,' answered Pinocchio, 'if I am to choose I should prefer to be set at liberty and to go home.'

'You are joking! Do you imagine that I would lose the opportunity of tasting such a rare fish? It is not every day, I assure you, that a puppet fish is caught in these waters. Leave it to me. I will fry you in the frying-pan with the other fish, and you will be quite satisfied. It is always a consolation to be fried in company.'

At this speech the unhappy Pinocchio began to cry and scream, and to implore for mercy; and he said, sobbing: 'How much better it would have been if I had gone to school! . . . I would listen to my companions and now I am paying for it! Oh! . . . Oh! . . . Oh!'

And he wriggled like an eel, and made indescribable efforts to slip out of the clutches of the green fisherman. But it was useless: the fisherman took a long strip of rush, and having bound his hands and feet as if he had been a sausage he threw him into the pan with the other fish.

He then fetched a wooden bowl full of flour and began to flour them each in turn, and as soon as they were ready he threw them into the frying-pan.

The first to dance in the boiling oil were the poor whiting; the bass followed, then the sardines, then the soles, then the anchovies, then the mullet, and at last it was Pinocchio's turn. Seeing himself so near death, and such a horrible death, he was so frightened, and trembled so violently, that he had neither voice nor breath left for further entreaties.

But the poor boy implored with his eyes! The green fisherman, however, without caring in the least, plunged him five or six times in the flour, until he was white from head to foot, and looked like a puppet made of plaster.

He then took him by the head, and . . .

XXIX

He returns to the Fairy's house. She promises him that the following day he shall cease to be a puppet and shall become a boy. Grand breakfast of coffee and milk to celebrate this great event.

Just as the fisherman was on the point of throwing Pinocchio into the frying-pan a large dog entered the cave, enticed by the strong and savoury odour of fried fish.

'Get out!' shouted the fisherman threateningly, holding the floured puppet in his hand.

But the poor dog, who was as hungry as a wolf, whined and wagged his tail as much as to say:

'Give me a mouthful of fish and I will leave you in peace.'

'Get out, I tell you!' repeated the fisherman, and he stretched out his leg to give him a kick.

But the dog who, when he was really hungry, would not stand trifling, turned upon him, growling and showing his terrible fangs.

At that moment a little feeble voice was heard in the cave saying entreatingly:

'Save me, Alidoro! If you don't save me I shall be fried!'

The dog recognized Pinocchio's voice, and to his extreme surprise perceived that it proceeded from the floured bundle that the fisherman held in his hand.

So what do you think he did? He made a spring, seized the

bundle in his mouth, and holding it gently between his teeth he rushed out of the cave and was gone like a flash of lightning.

The fisherman, furious at seeing a fish he was so anxious to eat snatched from him, ran after the dog; but he had not gone many steps when he was seized by a fit of coughing and had to give it up.

Alidoro, when he had reached the path that led to the village, stopped, and put his friend Pinocchio gently on the ground.

'How much I have to thank you for!' said the puppet.

'There is no necessity,' replied the dog. 'You saved me, and one good turn deserves another. We must all help each other in this world.'

'But how came you to come to the cave?'

'I was lying on the shore more dead than alive when the wind brought to me the smell of fried fish. The smell excited my appetite, and I followed it up. If I had arrived a second later——'

'Don't talk of it!' groaned Pinocchio, who was still trembling with fright. 'Don't talk of it! If you had arrived a second later I should by this time have been fried, eaten, and digested. Brrr! . . . it makes me shudder only to think of it!'

Alidoro, laughing, extended his right paw to the puppet, who shook it heartily in token of great friendship, and they then separated.

The dog took the road home; and Pinocchio, left alone, went to a cottage not far off, and said to a little old man who was warming himself in the sun:

'Tell me, good man, do you know anything of a poor boy called Eugene who was wounded in the head?'

'The boy was brought by some fishermen to this cottage, and now——'

'And now he is dead!' interrupted Pinocchio with great sorrow.

'No, he is alive, and has gone back to his own home.'

'Not really? not really?' cried the puppet, dancing with delight. 'Then the wound was not serious?'

'It might have been very serious and even fatal,' answered the little old man, 'for they threw a thick book bound in cardboard at his head.'

He . . . seized the bundle in his mouth

'And who threw it at him?'

'One of his schoolfellows, a certain Pinocchio.'

'And who is this Pinocchio?' asked the puppet, pretending not to know.

'They say that he is a bad boy, a vagabond, a regular ne'er-do-well.'

'Lies! All lies!'

'Do you know this Pinocchio?'

'By sight,' answered the puppet.

'And what is your opinion of him?' asked the little man.

'He seems to me to be a very good boy, anxious to learn, and obedient and affectionate to his father and family.'

Whilst the puppet was firing off all these lies he touched his nose and perceived that it had lengthened by a few inches. Very much alarmed he began to cry out:

'Don't believe, good man, what I have been telling you. I know Pinocchio very well, and I can assure you that he is really a very bad boy, disobedient and idle, who instead of going to school runs off with his school friends to have a good time.'

He had hardly finished speaking when his nose became shorter, and returned to the same size that it was before.

'And why are you all covered with white?' asked the old man suddenly.

'I will tell you. . . . Without meaning to I brushed against a wall which had been freshly whitewashed,' answered the puppet, ashamed to confess that he had been floured like a fish prepared for the frying-pan.

'And what have you done with your jacket, your trousers, and your cap?'

'I met with robbers who took them from me. Tell me, good old man, could you perhaps give me some clothes to return home in?'

'My boy, as to clothes, I have nothing but a little sack in which I keep beans. If you want it, take it; there it is.'

Pinocchio did not wait to be told twice. He took the sack at once, and with a pair of scissors he cut a hole at the end and at each side, and put it on like a shirt. And with this slight clothing he set off for the village.

But as he went he did not feel at all comfortable—so little so, indeed, that at each step forward he took another backwards, and he said, talking to himself:

'How shall I ever show myself to my good little Fairy? What will she say when she sees me? . . . Will she forgive me for this second escapade? . . . I bet that she will not forgive me! Oh, I am sure that she will not forgive me! . . . And it serves me right, for I am a rascal. I am always promising to be good, and I never keep my word!'

When he reached the village it was night and very dark. A storm had come on, and as the rain was coming down in torrents he went straight to the Fairy's house, determined to knock at the door, and hoping to be let in.

But when he was there his courage failed him, and instead of knocking he ran away some twenty paces. He returned to the door a second time, but could not make up his mind; he came back a third time, still he dared not; the fourth time he laid hold of the knocker and, trembling all over, he gave a tiny knock.

He waited and waited. At last, after half an hour had passed, a window on the top floor was opened—the house was four storeys high—and Pinocchio saw a big Snail with a lighted candle on her head looking out. She called to him:

'Who is there at this time of night?'

'Is the Fairy at home?' asked the puppet.

'The Fairy is asleep and must not be awakened; but who are you?'

'It's me!'

'Who is me?'

'Pinocchio.'

'And who is Pinocchio?'

'The puppet who lives in the Fairy's house.'

'Ah, I understand!' said the Snail. 'Wait for me there. I will come down and open the door directly.'

'Be quick, for pity's sake, for I am dying of cold.'

'My boy, I am a snail, and snails are never in a hurry.'

An hour passed, and then two, and the door was still shut. Pinocchio, who was wet through, and trembling from cold and fear, at last took courage and knocked again, and this time he knocked louder.

At this second knock a window on the lower storey opened, and the same Snail appeared at it.

'My pretty little Snail,' cried Pinocchio from the street, 'I have been waiting for two hours! And two hours on such a bad night seem longer than two years. Be quick, for pity's sake.'

'My boy,' answered the calm, phlegmatic little animal—'my boy, I am a snail, and snails are never in a hurry.'

And the window was shut again.

Shortly afterwards midnight struck; then one o'clock, then two o'clock, and the door was still closed.

Pinocchio at last, losing all patience, seized the knocker in a rage, intending to give a blow that would resound through the house. But the knocker, which was iron, turned suddenly into an eel, and slipping out of his hands disappeared in the stream of water that ran down the middle of the street.

'Ah! so that's it!' shouted Pinocchio, blind with rage. 'Since the knocker has disappeared I will kick instead with all my might.'

And drawing a little back he gave a tremendous kick against the house door. The blow was indeed so violent that his foot went through the wood and stuck; and when he tried to draw it back again it was quite useless, for it remained fixed like a nail that has been hammered down.

Think of poor Pinocchio! He was obliged to spend the remainder of the night with one foot on the ground and the other in the air.

The following morning at daybreak the door was at last opened. That clever little Snail had taken only nine hours to come down from the fourth storey to the house door. She must have been dripping with perspiration.

'What are you doing with your foot stuck in the door?' she asked the puppet, laughing.

'It was an accident. Do try, pretty little Snail, if you can release me from this torture.'

'My boy, that is the work of a carpenter, and I have never been a carpenter.'

'Beg the Fairy from me!'

'The Fairy is asleep and must not be wakened.'

'But what do you suppose that I can do all day nailed to this door?'

'Amuse yourself by counting the ants that pass down the street.'

'Bring me at least something to eat, for I am fainting with hunger.'

'At once,' said the Snail.

The Snail returned carrying a silver tray

In fact, after three hours and a half she returned to Pinocchio carrying a silver tray on her head. The tray contained a loaf of bread, a roast chicken, and four ripe apricots.

'Here is the breakfast that the Fairy has sent you,' said the Snail.

The puppet felt very much comforted at the sight of these

good things. But when he began to eat them, what was his dis-
gust at finding that the bread was plaster, the chicken cardboard,
and the four apricots painted alabaster!

He wanted to cry. In his desperation he tried to throw away
the tray and all that was on it; but instead, either from grief or
exhaustion, he fainted away.

When he came to himself he found that he was lying on a
sofa, and the Fairy was beside him.

'I will forgive you once more,' the Fairy said, 'but woe to
you if you behave badly a third time!'

Pinocchio promised, and swore that he would study, and
that for the future he would always behave well.

And he kept his word for the remainder of the year. Indeed,
at the examinations before the holidays, he had the honour of being the first in the school, and his behaviour in general was so
satisfactory and praise-worthy that the Fairy was very much
pleased, and said to him:

'To-morrow your wish shall be gratified.'

'And that is?'

'To-morrow you shall cease to be a wooden puppet, and you
shall become a boy.'

No one who had not witnessed it could ever imagine Pinocchio's joy at this long-sighed-for good fortune. All his schoolfellows were to be invited for the following day to a grand
breakfast at the Fairy's house, that they might celebrate together
the great event. The Fairy had prepared two hundred cups
of coffee and milk, and four hundred rolls cut and buttered on
both sides. The day promised to be most happy and delightful, but . . .

Unfortunately in the lives of puppets there is always a 'but'
that spoils everything.

XXX

PINOCCHIO, INSTEAD OF BECOMING A BOY, IS PERSUADED TO GO WITH HIS FRIEND CANDLEWICK TO TOYLAND.

PINOCCHIO, AS WAS NATURAL, asked the Fairy's permission to go round the town to give the invitations; and the Fairy said to him:

'Go if you like and invite your school friends for breakfast to-morrow, but remember to return home before dark. Have you understood?'

'I promise to be back in an hour,' answered the puppet.

'Take care, Pinocchio! Boys are always very ready to promise; but generally they are little given to keeping their word.'

'But I am not like other boys. When I say a thing I do it.'

'We shall see. If you are disobedient, so much the worse for you.'

'Why?'

'Because boys who do not listen to the advice of those who know more than they do always meet with some misfortune or other.'

'I have experienced that,' said Pinocchio. 'But I shall never make that mistake again.'

'We shall see if that is true.'

Without saying more the puppet took leave of his good Fairy, who was like a mamma to him, and went out of the house singing and dancing.

In less than an hour all his friends were invited. Some

accepted at once heartily; others at first required pressing; but
when they heard that the rolls to be eaten with the coffee were to
be buttered on both sides they ended by saying:

'We 'll come as well, to please you.'

Now I must tell you that amongst Pinocchio's friends and
schoolfellows there was one that he greatly preferred and was
very fond of. This boy's name was Romeo; but he always went
by the nickname of Candlewick, because he was so thin, straight,
and bright like the new wick of a little night-light.

Candlewick was the laziest and the naughtiest boy in the
school; but Pinocchio was devoted to him. He had indeed
gone at once to his house to invite him to the breakfast, but
he had not found him. He returned a second time, but Candlewick was not there. He went a third time, but it was in vain.
Where could he search for him? He looked here, there, and
everywhere, and at last he saw him hiding in the porch of a peasant's cottage.

'What are you doing there?' asked Pinocchio, coming up
to him.

'I am waiting for midnight, to start——'

'Why, where are you going?'

'Very far, very far, very far away.'

'And I have been three times to your house to look for you.'

'What do you want with me?'

'Do you not know the great event? Have you not heard of
my good fortune?'

'What is it?'

'To-morrow I cease to be a puppet, and I become a boy like
you, and like all the other boys.'

'Much good may it do you.'

'To-morrow, therefore, I expect you to breakfast at my
house.'

'But when I tell you that I am going away to-night?'

'At what time?'

'In a little while.'

'And where are you going?'

'I am going to live in a country . . . the most delightful country in the world: a real land of Plenty.'

'And what is its name?'

'It is called Toyland. Why don't you come too?'

'I? No, never!'

'You are wrong, Pinocchio. Believe me, if you do not come you will be sorry for it. Where could you find a better country for us boys? There are no schools there; there are no masters; there are no books. In that delightful land nobody ever studies. There is no school on Thursdays; and every week consists of six Thursdays and one Sunday. Only think, the autumn holidays begin on the 1st of January and finish on the last day of December. That is the country for me! That is what all civilized countries should be like!'

'But how do you pass the days in Toyland?'

'In games and fun from morning till night. When night comes you go to bed, and begin all over again in the morning. What do you think of that?'

'Hum! . . .' said Pinocchio; and he shook his head slightly as much as to say: 'That's the life for me!'

'Well, will you go with me? Yes or no? Make up your mind at once.'

'No, no, no, and again no. I promised my good Fairy to become a well-behaved boy, and I will keep my word. And as I see that the sun is setting I must leave you at once and run away. Good-bye, and a pleasant journey to you.'

'Where are you rushing off to in such a hurry?'

'Home. My good Fairy wishes me to be back before dark.'

'Wait another two minutes.'

'It will make me too late.'

'Only two minutes.'

'And if the Fairy scolds me?'

'Let her scold. When she has scolded well she will hold her tongue,' said that rascal Candlewick.

'And what are you going to do? Are you going alone or with friends?'

'Alone? We shall be more than a hundred boys.'

'Are you going on foot?'

'A coach is passing by shortly which is to take me to that happy country.'

'What wouldn't I give for the coach to pass by now!'

'Why?'

'That I might see you all start together.'

'Stay here a little longer and you will see us.'

'No, no, I must go home.'

'Wait another two minutes.'

'I have already delayed too long. The Fairy will be anxious about me.'

'Poor Fairy! Is she afraid that the bats will eat you?'

'But now,' continued Pinocchio, 'are you really certain that there are no schools in that country?'

'Not even the shadow of one.'

'And no teachers either?'

'Not one.'

'And no one is ever made to study?'

'Never, never, never!'

'What a delightful country!' said Pinocchio, his mouth watering. 'What a delightful country! I have never been there but I can quite imagine it——'

'Why will you not come also?'

'It is useless to tempt me. I promised my good Fairy to become a sensible boy, and I will not break my word.'

'Good-bye, then, and give my greetings to all the boys at school, and also to those in the higher schools, if you meet them in the street.'

'Good-bye, Candlewick: a pleasant journey to you, amuse yourself, and think sometimes of your friends.'

Thus saying the puppet made two steps to go, but then stopped, and turning to his friend he inquired:

'But are you quite certain that in that country all the weeks consist of six Thursdays and one Sunday?'

'Most certain.'

'But do you know for certain that the holidays begin on the 1st of January and finish on the last day of December?'

'Assuredly.'

'What a delightful country!' repeated Pinocchio, looking enchanted. Then, with a resolute air, he added in a great hurry:

'This time really good-bye, and a pleasant journey to you.'

'Good-bye.'

'When do you start?'

'Shortly.'

'What a delightful country! . . . What a delightful country!'

'What a pity! If really it wanted only an hour to the time of
your start I should be almost tempted to wait.'

'And the Fairy?'

'It's already late. . . . If I return home an hour sooner or an
hour later it will be all the same.'

'Poor Pinocchio! And if the Fairy scolds you?'

'I must have patience! I'll let her scold. When she has
scolded well she will hold her tongue.'

In the meantime night had come on and it was quite dark.
Suddenly they saw in the distance a small light moving . . . and
they heard a noise of talking, and the sound of a trumpet, but so
small and feeble that it resembled the hum of a mosquito.

'Here it is!' shouted Candlewick, jumping to his feet.

'What is it?' asked Pinocchio in a whisper.

'It is the coach coming to take me. Now will you come, yes
or no?'

'But is it really true,' asked the puppet, 'that in that country boys are never obliged to study?'

'Never, never, never!'

'What a delightful country! . . . What a delightful country! . . . What a delightful country!'

XXXI

AFTER FIVE MONTHS' RESIDENCE IN THE
LAND OF PLENTY, PINOCCHIO, TO HIS
GREAT ASTONISHMENT, GROWS A
BEAUTIFUL PAIR OF DONKEY'S EARS, AND
HE BECOMES A LITTLE DONKEY,
TAIL AND ALL.

AT LAST THE COACH ARRIVED; and it arrived without making the slightest noise, for its wheels were bound round with tow and rags.

It was drawn by twelve pairs of donkeys, all the same size but of different colours.

Some were grey, some white, some brindled like pepper and salt, and others had large stripes of yellow and blue.

But the most extraordinary thing was this: the twelve pairs, that is, the twenty-four donkeys, instead of being shod like other beasts of burden, had on their feet men's boots made of white kid.

And the coachman?

Picture to yourself a little man broader than he was long, flabby and greasy like a lump of butter, with a small round face like an orange, a little mouth that was always laughing, and a soft caressing voice like a cat's when she is trying to insinuate herself into the good graces of the mistress of the house.

All the boys as soon as they saw him lost their hearts to him,

And the coachman?

and vied with each other in taking places in his coach to be conducted to the true land of Plenty, known on the geographical map by the attractive name of Toyland.

The coach was in fact quite full of boys between eight and twelve years old, heaped one upon another like herrings in a barrel. They were uncomfortable, packed close together, and could hardly breathe: but nobody said Oh!—nobody grumbled. The consolation of knowing that in a few hours they would reach a country where there were no books, no schools, and no teachers, made them so happy and resigned that they felt neither fatigue nor inconvenience, neither hunger, nor thirst, nor want of sleep.

As soon as the coach had drawn up the little man turned to Candlewick, and smirking and smiling said to him:

'Tell me, my fine boy, would you also like to go to that fortunate country?'

'I certainly want to go.'

'But I must warn you, my dear child, that there is not a place left in the coach. You can see for yourself that it is quite full——'

'No matter,' replied Candlewick; 'if there is no place inside, I will manage to sit on the shaft.'

And giving a leap he seated himself astride on the shaft.

'And you, my dear! . . .' said the little man, turning in a flattering manner to Pinocchio. 'What do you intend to do? Are you coming with us, or are you going to remain behind?'

'I remain behind,' answered Pinocchio. 'I am going home. I intend to study and to earn a good character at school, as all well-conducted boys do.'

'Much good may it do you!'

'Pinocchio!' called out Candlewick, 'listen to me: come with us and we shall have such fun.'

'No, no, no!'

'Come with us, and we shall have such fun,' cried four other voices from the inside of the coach.

'Come with us, and we shall have such fun,' shouted in chorus a hundred voices from the inside of the coach.

'But if I come with you, what will my good Fairy say?' said the puppet, who was beginning to yield.

'Do not trouble your head with melancholy thoughts. Consider only that we are going to a country where we shall be at liberty to run wild from morning till night.'

Pinocchio did not answer; but he sighed: he sighed again: he sighed for the third time, and he said finally:

'Make a little room for me, for I am coming too.'

'The places are all full,' replied the little man; 'but to show you how welcome you are you shall have my seat on the box——'

'And you?'

'Oh, I will go on foot.'

'No, indeed, I could not allow that. I would rather get on to one of these donkeys,' cried Pinocchio.

Approaching the right-hand donkey of the first pair he attempted to mount him, but the animal turned on him, and giving him a great blow in the stomach rolled him over with his legs in the air.

You can imagine the loud and impudent laughter of all the boys who witnessed this scene.

But the little man did not laugh. He approached the rebellious donkey and, pretending to give him a kiss, bit off half of his ear.

Pinocchio in the meantime had got up from the ground in a fury, and with a spring he seated himself on the poor animal's back. And he sprang so well that the boys stopped laughing and began to shout: 'Hurrah, Pinocchio!' and they clapped their hands and applauded him as if they would never finish.

But the donkey suddenly kicked up its hind legs, and backing violently threw the poor puppet into the middle of the road on to a heap of stones.

The roars of laughter began again: but the little man, instead of laughing, felt such sympathy for the restive ass that he kissed him again, and as he did so he bit half of his other ear clean off. He then said to the puppet:

'Mount him now without fear. That little donkey had got some whim into his head; but I whispered two little words into his ears which have, I hope, made him gentle and reasonable.'

Pinocchio mounted, and the coach started. Whilst the donkeys were galloping and the coach was rattling over the stones of the high road, the puppet thought that he heard a low voice that was scarcely intelligible saying to him:

'Poor fool! you would follow your own way, but you will repent it!'

Pinocchio, feeling almost frightened, looked from side to side to try and discover where these words could come from: but he saw nobody. The donkeys galloped, the coach rattled, the boys inside slept, Candlewick snored liked a dormouse, and the little man seated on the box sang between his teeth:

'During the night all sleep,
But I sleep never . . .'

After they had gone another mile Pinocchio heard the same little low voice saying to him:

'Bear it in mind, simpleton! Boys who refuse to study, and turn their backs upon books, schools, and teachers, to pass their time in play and amusement, sooner or later come to a bad end. . . . I know it by experience . . . and I can tell you. A day will come when you will weep as I am weeping now . . . but then it will be too late!'

On hearing these words whispered very softly the puppet, more frightened than ever, sprang down from the back of his donkey and went and took hold of his mouth.

Imagine his surprise when he found that the donkey was crying . . . and he was crying like a boy!

'Hey, Sir Coachman!' cried Pinocchio to the little man, 'here is an extraordinary thing! This donkey is crying.'

'Let him cry; he will laugh when he is a bridegroom.'

'But have you by chance taught him to talk?'

'No; but he spent three years in a company of performing dogs, and he learnt to mutter a few words.'

'Poor beast!'

'Come, come,' said the little man, 'don't let us waste time in seeing a donkey cry. Mount him, and let us go on: the night is cold and the road is long.'

Pinocchio obeyed without another word. In the morning about daybreak they arrived safely at Toyland.

It was a country unlike any other country in the world. The population was composed entirely of boys. The oldest were fourteen, and the youngest scarcely eight years old. In the streets there was such merriment, noise, and shouting, that it was enough to turn anybody's head. There were troops of boys everywhere. Some were playing with nuts, some with battle-dores, some with balls. Some rode bicycles, others wooden horses. A party were playing at hide and seek, a few were chasing each other. Boys dressed as clowns were eating lighted tow; some were reciting, some singing, some leaping. Some were amusing themselves with walking on their hands with their feet in the air; others were trundling hoops, or strutting about dressed as generals, wearing paper helmets and commanding a squadron of cardboard soldiers. Some were laughing, some shouting, some were calling out; others clapped their hands, or whistled, or clucked like a hen who has just laid an egg. To sum it all up, it was such a pandemonium, such a bedlam, such an uproar, that not to be deafened it would have been necessary to stuff one's ears with cotton wool. In every square, canvas theatres had been erected, and they were crowded with boys from morning till evening. On the walls of the houses there were inscriptions written in charcoal: 'Long live toys and games; no more schools; down with arithmetic'; and other similar fine sentiments all in bad spelling.

Pinocchio, Candlewick, and the other boys who had made the journey with the little man, had scarcely set foot in the town before they were in the thick of the tumult, and I need not tell you that in a few minutes they had made acquaintance with everybody. Where could you find happier or more contented boys?

In the midst of perpetual games and every variety of amusement, the hours, the days, and the weeks passed like lightning.

'Oh, what a delightful life!' said Pinocchio, whenever by chance he met Candlewick.

'You see, I was right,' replied the other. 'And to think that you did not want to come! To think that you had taken it into your head to return home to your Fairy, and to lose your time in studying! . . . If you are at this moment free from the bother of books and school, you must acknowledge that you owe it to me, to my advice, and to my persuasions. It is only friends who know how to render such great services.'

'It is true, Candlewick! If I am now a really happy boy it is all your doing. But do you know what the teacher used to say when he talked to me of you? He always said to me: "Do not go about with that rascal Candlewick, for he is a bad companion, and will only lead you into mischief!" '

'Poor man!' replied the other, shaking his head. 'I know only too well that he disliked me, and amused himself by slandering me; but I am generous and I forgive him!'

'How noble you are!' said Pinocchio, embracing his friend affectionately, and kissing him on the forehead.

This delightful life had gone on for five months. The days had been entirely spent in play and amusement, without a thought of books or school, when one morning Pinocchio awoke to a most disagreeable surprise that put him into a very bad humour.

XXXII

PINOCCHIO GETS DONKEY'S EARS; AND THEN HE BECOMES A REAL LITTLE DONKEY AND BEGINS TO BRAY.

W HAT was this surprise?

I will tell you, my dear little readers. The surprise was that Pinocchio when he awoke scratched his head; and in scratching his head he discovered . . . Can't you guess the least little bit what he discovered?

He discovered to his great astonishment that his ears had grown by several inches.

You know that the puppet from his birth had always had very small ears—so small that they were not visible to the naked eye. You can imagine then what he felt when he found that during the night his ears had become so long that they seemed like two brooms.

He went at once in search of a glass that he might look at himself, but not being able to find one he filled the basin of his wash-stand with water, and he saw reflected what he certainly would never have wished to see. He saw his head embellished with a magnificent pair of donkey's ears!

He saw his head embelished with . . . donkey's ears

Only think of poor Pinocchio's sorrow, shame, and despair!

He began to cry and roar, and he beat his head against the wall; but the more he cried the longer his ears grew: they grew, and grew, and became hairy towards the points.

At the sound of his loud outcries a beautiful little Marmot that lived on the first floor came into the room. Seeing the puppet in such grief she asked earnestly:

'What has happened to you, my dear fellow lodger?'

'I am ill, my dear little Marmot, very ill . . . and of an illness that frightens me. Do you understand counting a pulse?'

'A little.'

'Then feel and see if by chance I have got fever.'

The little Marmot raised her right forepaw; and after having felt Pinocchio's pulse she said to him, sighing:

'My friend, I am grieved to be obliged to give you bad news!'

'What is it?'

'You have got a very bad fever!'

'What fever is it?'

'It is donkey fever.'

'That is a fever that I do not understand,' said the puppet, but he understood it only too well.

'Then I will explain it to you,' said the Marmot. 'You must know that in two or three hours you will be no longer a puppet, or a boy.'

'Then what shall I be?'

'In two or three hours you will become really and truly a little donkey, like those that draw carts and carry cabbages and salad to market.'

'Oh! unfortunate that I am! unfortunate that I am!' cried Pinocchio, seizing his two ears with his hands, and pulling them and tearing them furiously as if they had been someone else's ears.

'My dear boy,' said the Marmot, by way of consoling him, 'what can you do to prevent it? It is destiny. It is written in the decrees of wisdom that all boys who are lazy, and who take a dislike to books, to schools, and to teachers, and who pass their time in amusement, games, and diversions, must end sooner or later by becoming transformed into so many little donkeys.'

'But is it really so?' asked the puppet, sobbing.

'It is indeed only too true! And tears are now useless. You should have thought of it sooner!'

'But it was not my fault: believe me, little Marmot, the fault was all Candlewick's!'

'And who is this Candlewick?'

'One of my schoolfellows. I wanted to return home: I wanted to be obedient. I wished to study and to earn a good character . . . but Candlewick said to me: "Why should you bother yourself by studying? Why should you go to school? . . . Come with us instead to Toyland: there we shall none of us have to learn: there we shall amuse ourselves from morning to night, and we shall always be merry." '

'And why did you follow the advice of that false friend? of that bad companion?'

'Why? . . . Because, my dear little Marmot, I am a puppet with no sense . . . and with no heart. Ah! if I had had the least heart I should never have left that good Fairy who loved me like a mamma, and who had done so much for me! . . . and I should be no longer a puppet . . . for I should by this time have become a little boy like so many others! But if I meet Candlewick, woe to him! He shall hear what I think of him!'

And he turned to go out. But when he reached the door he remembered his donkey's ears, and feeling ashamed to show them in public, what do you think he did? He took a big cotton cap, and putting it on his head, he pulled it well down over the point of his nose.

He then set out and went everywhere in search of Candlewick. He looked for him in the streets, in the squares, in the little theatres, in every possible place; but he could not find him. He inquired for him of everybody he met, but no one had seen him.

He then went to seek him at his house; and having reached the door he knocked.

'Who is there?' asked Candlewick from within.

'It's me!' answered the puppet.

'Wait a moment and I will let you in.'

After half an hour the door was opened, and imagine Pinocchio's feelings when upon going into the room he saw his friend Candlewick with a big cotton cap on his head which came down over his nose.

At the sight of the cap Pinocchio felt almost consoled, and thought to himself:

'Has my friend got the same illness that I have? Is he also suffering from donkey fever?'

And pretending to have noticed nothing he asked him, smiling:

'How are you, my dear Candlewick?'

'Very well; as happy as a mouse in a Parmesan cheese.'

'Are you saying that seriously?'

'Why should I tell you a lie?'

'Excuse me; but why, then, do you keep that cotton cap on your head which covers up your ears?'

'The doctor ordered me to wear it because I have hurt this knee. And you, dear puppet, why have you got on that cotton cap pulled down over your nose?'

'The doctor prescribed it because I have grazed my foot.'

'Oh, poor Pinocchio!'

'Oh, poor Candlewick!'

After these words a long silence followed, during which the two friends did nothing but look mockingly at each other.

At last the puppet said in a soft persuasive voice to his companion:

'Satisfy my curiosity, my dear Candlewick: have you ever suffered from disease of the ears?'

'Never! . . . And you?'

'Never! Only since this morning one of my ears aches.'

'Mine is also paining me.'

'You also? . . . And which of your ears hurts you?'

'Both of them. And you?'

'Both of them. Can we have got the same illness?'

'I fear so.'

'Will you do me a kindness, Candlewick?'

'Willingly! With all my heart.'

'Will you let me see your ears?'

'Why not? But first, my dear Pinocchio, I should like to see yours.'

'No; you must be the first.'

'No, my friend. First you and then me!'

'Well,' said the puppet, 'let us come to an agreement like good friends.'

'Let us hear it.'

'We will both take off our caps at the same moment. Do you agree?'

'I agree.'

'Then attention!'

And Pinocchio began to count in a loud voice:

'One! Two! Three!'

At the word 'three!' the two boys took off their caps and threw them into the air.

And then a scene followed that would seem incredible if it was not true. That is, that when Pinocchio and Candlewick discovered that they were both struck with the same misfortune, instead of feeling full of mortification and grief, they began to prick their ungainly ears and to play a thousand antics, and they ended by going into bursts of laughter.

And they laughed, and laughed, and laughed, until they had to hold themselves together. But in the midst of their merriment Candlewick suddenly stopped, staggered, and changing colour said to his friend:

'Help, help, Pinocchio!'

'What is the matter with you?'

'Alas, I cannot stand upright any longer.'

'No more can I,' exclaimed Pinocchio, tottering and beginning to cry.

And whilst they were talking they both doubled up and began to run round the room on their hands and feet. And as they ran their hands became hoofs, their faces lengthened into muzzles, and their backs became covered with a light grey hairy coat sprinkled with black.

But do you know what was the worst moment for these two wretched boys? The worst and the most humiliating moment was when their tails grew. Vanquished by shame and sorrow they wept and lamented their fate.

Oh, if they had but been wiser! But instead of sighs and lamentations they could only bray like assess; and they brayed loudly and said in chorus: 'Hee-haw, hee-haw!'

Whilst this was going on someone knocked at the door, and a voice outside said:

'Open the door! I am the little man, I am the coachman, who brought you to this country. Open at once, or it will be the worse for you!'

XXXIII

PINOCCHIO, HAVING BECOME A GENUINE
LITTLE DONKEY, IS TAKEN TO BE SOLD,
AND IS BOUGHT BY THE RINGMASTER OF A
CIRCUS TO BE TAUGHT TO DANCE, AND TO
JUMP THROUGH HOOPS: BUT ONE EVENING
HE LAMES HIMSELF, AND THEN HE IS
BOUGHT BY A MAN WHO PURPOSES TO
MAKE A DRUM OF HIS SKIN.

FINDING THAT THE DOOR remained shut the little man burst
it open with a violent kick, and coming into the room he said to
Pinocchio and Candlewick with his usual little laugh:

'Well done, boys! You brayed well, and I recognized you by
your voices. That is why I am here.'

At these words the two little donkeys were quite stupefied,
and stood with their heads down, their ears lowered, and their
tails between their legs.

At first the little man stroked and caressed them; then taking
out a curry-comb he curry-combed them well. And when by this
process he had polished them till they shone like two mirrors, he
put a halter round their necks and led them to the market-place,
in hopes of selling them and making a good profit.

And indeed buyers were not wanting. Candlewick was

bought by a peasant whose donkey had died the previous day. Pinocchio was sold to the Ringmaster of a circus which included clowns and tight-rope dancers, who bought him that he might teach him to leap and to dance with the other animals belonging to the company.

And now, my little readers, you will have understood the fine trade that little man pursued. The wicked little monster, who had a face all milk and honey, made frequent journeys round the world with his coach. As he went along he collected, with promises and flattery, all the idle boys who had taken an aversion to books and school. As soon as his coach was full he conducted them to Toyland, that they might pass their time in games, in uproar, and in amusement. When these poor deluded boys, from continual play and no study, had become so many little donkeys, he took possession of them with great delight and satisfaction, and carried them off to the fairs and markets to be sold. And in this way in a few years he had made heaps of money and had become a millionaire.

What became of Candlewick I do not know; but I do know that Pinocchio from the very first day had to endure a very hard, laborious life.

When he was put into his stall his master filled the manger with straw; but Pinocchio, having tried a mouthful, spat it out again.

Then his master, grumbling, filled the manger with hay; but neither did the hay please him.

'Ah!' exclaimed his master in a passion. 'Hay doesn't please you either? Leave it to me, my fine donkey; if you are so full of fancies I will find a way to cure you!'

And by way of correcting him he struck his legs with his whip.

Pinocchio began to cry and to bray with pain, and he said, braying:

'Hee-haw, I can't digest straw!'

'Then eat hay!' said his master, who understood perfectly the donkey dialect.

'Hee-haw, hay gives me a pain in my stomach.'

'Do you mean to say that a little donkey like you must be

fed on breasts of chickens, and capons in aspic?' asked his master, getting more and more angry, and whipping him again.

At this second whipping Pinocchio prudently held his tongue and said nothing more.

The stable was then shut and Pinocchio was left alone. He had not eaten for many hours, and he began to yawn with hunger. And when he yawned he opened a mouth that seemed as wide as an oven.

At last, finding nothing else in the manger, he resigned himself and chewed a little hay; and after he had chewed it well he shut his eyes and swallowed it.

'This hay is not bad,' he said to himself; 'but how much better it would have been if I had gone on with my studies! . . . Instead of hay I might now be eating a hunch of new bread and a fine slice of sausage! But I must have patience!'

The next morning when he woke he looked in the manger for a little more hay; but he found none, for he had eaten it all during the night.

Then he took a mouthful of chopped straw; but whilst he was chewing it he had to acknowledge that the taste of chopped straw did not in the least resemble a savoury dish of macaroni or rice.

'But I must have patience!' he repeated as he went on chewing. 'May my example serve at least as a warning to all disobedient boys who do not want to study. Patience! . . . patience!'

'Patience indeed!' shouted his master, coming at that moment into the stable. 'Do you think, my little donkey, that I bought you only to give you food and drink? I bought you to make you work, and that you might earn money for me. Up, then, at once! you must come with me into the circus, and there I will teach you to jump through hoops, to go through frames of paper head foremost, to dance waltzes and polkas, and to stand upright on your hind legs.'

Poor Pinocchio, either by fair means or foul, had to learn all these fine things. But it took him three months before he had learnt them, and he got many a whipping that nearly took off his skin.

At last a day came when his master was able to announce

that he would give a really great show. The many-coloured plac-
ards stuck on the street corners were worded thus:

GRAND GALA PERFORMANCE
TO-NIGHT
THE USUAL AMAZING FEATS AND EQUESTRIAN EXERCISES
Executed by all the Artistes of the Company
With the added attraction of the famous
LITTLE DONKEY PINOCCHIO
known as
THE STAR OF THE DANCE
who will make his first appearance

The theatre will be brilliantly illuminated

On that evening, as you may imagine, an hour before the
play was to begin the theatre was crammed.

There was not a place to be had either in the pit or the stalls,
or in the boxes even, by paying their weight in gold.

The benches round the circus were crowded with children
and with boys of all ages, who were in a fever of impatience to
see the famous little donkey Pinocchio dance.

When the first part of the performance was over the ringmaster, dressed in a black coat, white tights, and big leather boots
that came above his knees, presented himself to the public, and
after making a profound bow he began with much solemnity the
following flamboyant speech:

'My honoured audience, ladies and gentlemen. I am your
humble servant, merely a passer-by in this illustrious city, but I
now have the honour, as well as the pleasure, of presenting to
this intelligent and distinguished audience a celebrated donkey
who has already had the honour of dancing before His Majesty
the Emperor, in all the principal courts of Europe.

'While I thank you I entreat you to give us the inspiring sup-
port of your presence and your indulgence.'

This speech was received with much laughter and applause;
but the applause redoubled and became tumultuous when the little donkey Pinocchio made his appearance in the middle of the
circus. He was decked out for the occasion. He had a new bridle
of polished leather with brass buckles and studs, and a white

camellia in each ear. His mane was divided and curled, and each curl was tied with bows of coloured ribbon. He had a girth of gold and silver round his body, and his tail was plaited with amaranth and blue velvet ribbons. He was, in fact, a little donkey with whom you could fall in love!

The ringmaster, in presenting him to the public, added these few words:

'My honoured audience! I am not here to tell you any falsehoods about the great difficulties that I have had in capturing and dominating this mammal while he was still grazing at liberty, from mountain to mountain, in the plains of the torrid zone. I beg you to note the wild rolling of his eyes, so that every means having been tried in vain to tame him, and to accustom him to the life of domestic quadrupeds, I have often had to resort to the language of the whip. But all my goodness to him, instead of gaining his affections, has, on the contrary, increased his viciousness. However, following the system of Gall, I discovered a bump in his cranium and the Faculty of Medicine in Paris has pronounced it to be the regenerating bulb of the hair and of the Pyrrhic dance. For this reason I have not only taught him to dance, but also to jump through hoops and through frames covered with paper. Admire him, and then pass your opinion on him! But before taking my leave of you, permit me, ladies and gentlemen, to invite you to the daily performance that will take place to-morrow evening; but in the event that the weather should threaten rain the performance will be postponed till to-morrow morning at eleven o'clock in the afternoon.'

Here the director made another profound bow; and then turning to Pinocchio he said:

'Courage, Pinocchio! Before you begin your feats make your bow to this distinguished audience—ladies, gentlemen, and children.'

Pinocchio obeyed, and bent both his knees till they touched the ground, and remained kneeling until the master, cracking his whip, shouted to him:

'At a foot-pace!'

Then the little donkey raised himself on his four legs and began to walk round the theatre, keeping at a foot-pace.

After a little the director cried:

'Trot!' and Pinocchio, obeying the order, changed to a trot.

'Canter!' and Pinocchio groke into a canter.

'Full gallop!' and Pinocchio went full gallop. But whilst he was going full speed like a racehorse the master, raising his arm in the air, fired off a pistol.

At the shot the little donkey, pretending to be wounded, fell his whole length in the circus, as if he was really dying.

As he got up from the ground amidst an outburst of applause, shouts, and clapping of hands, he naturally raised his head and looked up . . . and he saw in one of the boxes a beautiful lady who wore round her neck a thick gold chain from which hung a medallion. On the medallion was painted the portrait of a puppet.

'That is my portrait! . . . that lady is the Fairy!' said Pinocchio to himself, recognizing her immediately; and overcome with delight he tried to cry:

'Oh, my little Fairy! Oh, my little Fairy!'

But instead of these words a bray came from his throat, so hearty and so prolonged that all the spectators laughed, and more especially all the children who were in the theatre.

Then the ringmaster, to give him a lesson, and to make him understand that it is not good manners to bray before the public, gave him a blow on his nose with the handle of his whip.

The poor little donkey put his tongue out an inch, and licked his nose for at least five minutes, thinking perhaps that it would ease the pain he felt.

But what was his despair when, looking up a second time, he saw that the box was empty and that the Fairy had disappeared!

He thought he was going to die: his eyes filled with tears, and he began to weep. Nobody, however, noticed it, and least of all the master who, cracking his whip, shouted:

'Courage, Pinocchio! Now let the audience see how gracefully you can jump through the hoops.'

Pinocchio tried two or three times, but each time that he came in front of the hoop, instead of going through it he found it easier to go under it. At last he made a leap and went through it; but his right leg unfortunately caught in the hoop, and that caused him to fall on the other side doubled up in a heap on the ground.

When he got up he was lame, and it was only with great difficulty that he managed to go back to the stable.

'Bring out Pinocchio! We want the little donkey! Bring out the little donkey!' shouted all the boys in the theatre, touched and sorry for the sad accident.

But the little donkey was seen no more that evening.

The following morning the veterinary, that is, the animals' doctor, paid him a visit, and declared that he would remain lame for life.

The ringmaster then said to the stable-boy:

'What do you suppose I can do with a lame donkey? He

'Now let the audience see how gracefully you can
jump through the hoops'

would eat food without earning it. Take him to the market and sell him.'

When they reached the market a purchaser was found at once. He asked the stable-boy:

'How much do you want for that lame donkey?'

'Twenty lire.'

'I will give you twenty pence. Don't suppose that I am buying him to make use of; I am buying him solely for his skin. I see that his skin is very hard, and I intend to make a drum with it for the band of my village.'

I leave it to my readers to imagine poor Pinocchio's feelings when he heard that he was destined to become a drum!

As soon as the purchaser had paid his twenty pence he conducted the little donkey to the seashore. He then put a stone round his neck, and tying a rope, the end of which he held in his hand, round his leg, he gave him a sudden push and threw him into the water.

Pinocchio, weighed down by the stone, went at once to the bottom; and his owner, keeping tight hold of the cord, sat down quietly on a rock to wait until the little donkey was drowned, intending then to skin him.

XXXIV

PINOCCHIO, HAVING BEEN THROWN INTO
THE SEA, IS EATEN BY THE FISH, AND
BECOMES A PUPPET AS HE WAS BEFORE.
WHILST HE IS SWIMMING AWAY TO SAVE
HIS LIFE HE IS SWALLOWED BY THE
TERRIBLE SHARK.

AFTER PINOCCHIO had been fifty minutes under the water
his purchaser said aloud to himself:

'My poor little lame donkey must be quite drowned by this
time. I will therefore pull him out of the water, and I will make a
fine drum of his skin.'

And he began to haul in the rope that he had tied to the donkey's leg; and he hauled, and hauled, and hauled, until at last . . .
what do you think appeared above the water? Instead of a little
dead donkey he saw a live puppet, who was wriggling like an eel.

Seeing this wooden puppet the poor man thought he was
dreaming, and struck dumb with astonishment, he remained
with his mouth open and his eyes starting out of his head.

Having somewhat recovered from his first amazement he
asked in a quavering voice:

'And the little donkey that I threw into the sea? What has
become of him?'

'I am the little donkey!' said Pinocchio, laughing.

'You?'

'I.'

'Ah, you young scamp! Are you daring to make fun of me?'

'To make fun of you? Quite the contrary, my dear master; I am speaking seriously.'

The poor man thought he was dreaming

'But how can you, who, but a short time ago, were a little donkey, have become a wooden puppet, only from having been left in the water?'

'It must have been the effect of sea-water. The sea makes extraordinary changes.'

'Beware, puppet, beware! . . . Don't imagine that you can amuse yourself at my expense. It'll be the worse for you if I lose patience!'

'Well, master, do you wish to know the true story? If you will set my leg free I will tell it you.'

The good man, who was curious to hear the true story, immediately untied the knot that kept him bound; and Pinocchio, finding himself as free as a bird of the air, began as follows:

'You must know that I was once a puppet as I am now, and I was on the point of becoming a boy like the many that there are in the world. But instead, led away by my dislike to study and the advice of bad companions, I ran away from home . . . and one fine day when I awoke I found myself changed into a donkey with long ears . . . and a long tail! . . . What a disgrace it was to me!—a disgrace, dear master, that the blessed St. Anthony would not inflict even upon you! Taken to the market to be sold I was bought by the ringmaster of a circus company, who took it into his head to make a famous dancer of me, and a famous leaper through hoops. But one night during a performance I had a bad fall in the circus and lamed both my legs. Then the ringmaster, not knowing what to do with a lame donkey, sent me to be sold, and you were the purchaser!'

'Only too true! And I paid twenty pence for you. And now who will give me back my poor pennies?'

'And why did you buy me? You bought me to make a drum of my skin! . . . a drum!'

'Only too true! And now where shall I find another skin?'

'Don't despair, master. There are such a number of little donkeys in the world!'

'Tell me, you impertinent rascal, does your story end here?'

'No,' answered the puppet; 'I have another two words to say and then I shall have finished. After you had bought me you brought me to this place to kill me; and then, yielding to a feeling of compassion, you preferred to tie a stone round my neck and to throw me into the sea. This humane feeling does you great honour, and I shall always be grateful to you for it. But nevertheless, dear master, this time you made your calculations without considering the Fairy!'

'And who is this Fairy?'

'She is my mamma, and she resembles all other good mammas who care for their children, and who never lose sight of them, but help them lovingly, even when, on account of their foolishness and evil conduct, they deserve to be abandoned and left to themselves. Well, then, the good Fairy, as soon as she saw that I was in danger of drowning, sent immediately an immense shoal of fish, who, believing me really to be a little dead donkey, began to eat me. And what mouthfuls they took! I should never have thought that fish were greedier than boys! . . . Some ate my ears, some my muzzle, others my neck and mane, some the skin of my legs, some my coat . . . and amongst them there was a little fish so polite that he even condescended to eat my tail.'

'From this time forth,' said his purchaser, horrified, 'I swear that I will never touch fish. It would be too dreadful to open a mullet, or a fried whiting, and to find a donkey's tail inside!'

'I agree with you,' said the puppet, laughing. 'However, I must tell you that when the fish had finished eating the donkey's hide that covered me from head to foot, they naturally reached the bone . . . or rather the wood, for as you see I am made of the hardest wood. But after giving a few bites they soon discovered that I was not a dainty morsel and, disgusted with such indigestible food, they went off, some in one direction and some in another, without so much as saying thank you to me. And now, at last, I have told you how it was that when you pulled up the rope you found a live puppet instead of a dead donkey.'

'That 's enough of your story,' cried the man in a rage. 'I know only that I spent twenty pence to buy you, and I will have my money back. Shall I tell you what I will do? I will take you back to the market and I will sell you by weight as seasoned wood for lighting fires.'

'Sell me if you like; I am content,' said Pinocchio.

But as he said it he made a spring and plunged into the water. Swimming gaily away from the shore he called to his poor owner:

'Good-bye, master; if you should be in want of a skin to make a drum, remember me.'

And he laughed and went on swimming; and after a while he turned again and shouted louder:

'Good-bye, master; if you should be in want of a little well-seasoned wood for lighting the fire, remember me.'

In the twinkling of an eye he had swum so far off that he was scarcely visible. All that could be seen of him was a little black speck on the surface of the sea that from time to time lifted its legs out of the water and leapt and capered like a dolphin enjoying himself.

Whilst Pinocchio was swimming he knew not whither he saw in the midst of the sea a rock that seemed to be made of white marble, and on the summit there stood a beautiful little goat who bleated lovingly and made signs to him to approach.

But the most singular thing was this. The little goat's hair, instead of being white or black, or a mixture of two colours as is usual with other goats, was blue, and of a very vivid blue, greatly resembling the hair of the beautiful Little Girl.

I leave you to imagine how rapidly poor Pinocchio's heart began to beat. He swam with redoubled strength and energy towards the white rock; and he was already half-way when he saw, rising up out of the water and coming to meet him, the horrible head of a sea-monster. His wide-open cavernous mouth and his three rows of enormous teeth would have been terrifying to look at even in a picture.

And do you know what this sea-monster was?

This sea-monster was neither more nor less than that gigantic Shark who has been mentioned several times in this story, and who, for his slaughter and for his insatiable voracity, had been named the 'Attila of fish and fishermen.'

Only think of poor Pinocchio's terror at the sight of the monster. He tried to avoid it, to change his direction; he tried to escape; but that immense wide-open mouth came towards him with the swiftness of an arrow.

'Be quick, Pinocchio, for pity's sake,' cried the beautiful little goat, bleating.

And Pinocchio swam desperately with his arms, his chest, his legs, and his feet.

'Quick, Pinocchio, the monster is close upon you!'

And Pinocchio swam quicker than ever, and flew on with the rapidity of a bullet from a gun. He had nearly reached the rock, and the little goat, leaning over towards the sea, had stretched out her forelegs to help him out of the water!

But it was too late! The monster had overtaken him, and, drawing in his breath, he sucked in the poor puppet as he would have sucked a hen's egg; and he swallowed him with such violence and avidity that Pinocchio, in falling into the Shark's stomach, received such a blow that he remained unconscious for a quarter of an hour afterwards.

When he came to himself again after the shock he could not in the least imagine in what world he was. All round him it was quite dark, and the darkness was so black and so profound that it seemed to him that he had fallen head downwards into an inkstand full of ink. He listened, but he could hear no noise; only from time to time great gusts of wind blew in his face. At first he could not understand where the wind came from, but at last he discovered that it came out of the monster's lungs. For you must know that the Shark suffered very much from asthma, and when he breathed it was exactly as if a north wind was blowing.

Pinocchio at first tried to keep up his courage; but when he had one proof after another that he was really shut up in the body of this sea-monster he began to cry and scream and to sob out:

'Help! help! Oh, how unfortunate I am! Will nobody come to save me?'

'Who do you think could save you, unhappy wretch?' said a voice in the dark that sounded like a guitar out of tune.

'Who is speaking?' asked Pinocchio, frozen with terror.

'It's me! I am a poor Tunny who was swallowed by the Shark at the same time that you were. And what fish are you?'

'I have nothing in common with fish. I am a puppet.'

'Then if you are not a fish why did you let yourself be swallowed by the monster?'

'I didn't let myself be swallowed: it was the monster swallowed me! And now, what are we to do here in the dark?'

'Resign ourselves and wait until the Shark has digested us both.'

'But I do not want to be digested!' howled Pinocchio, beginning to cry again.

'Neither do I want to be digested,' added the Tunny; 'but I am enough of a philosopher to console myself by thinking that when one is born a Tunny it is more dignified to die in the water than in oil.'

'That's all nonsense!' cried Pinocchio.

'It is my opinion,' replied the Tunny; 'and opinions, so say the political Tunnies, ought to be respected.'

'To sum it all up . . . I want to get away from here . . . I want to escape.'

'Escape if you can!'

'Is this Shark who has swallowed us very big?' asked the puppet.

'Big! Why, only imagine, his body is two miles long without counting his tail.'

Whilst they were holding this conversation in the dark Pinocchio thought that he saw a light a long way off.

'What is that little light I see in the distance?' he asked.

'It is most likely some companion in misfortune who is waiting like us to be digested.'

'I will go and find him. Do you not think that it may by chance be some old fish who perhaps could show us how to escape?'

'I hope it may be so with all my heart, dear puppet.'

'Good-bye, Tunny.'

'Good-bye, puppet, and good fortune attend you.'

'Where shall we meet again?'

'Who can say? . . . It is better not even to think of it!'

XXXV

PINOCCHIO FINDS IN THE BODY OF THE SHARK ... WHOM DOES HE FIND? READ THIS CHAPTER AND YOU WILL KNOW.

PINOCCHIO, having taken leave of his friend the Tunny, began to grope his way in the dark through the body of the Shark, taking a step at a time in the direction of the light that he saw shining dimly at a great distance.

The farther he advanced the brighter became the light; and he walked and walked until at last he reached it: and when he reached it ... what did he find? I will give you a thousand guesses. He found a little table spread out, and on it a lighted candle stuck into a green glass bottle, and seated at the table was a little old man. He was eating some live fish, and they were so very much alive that whilst he was eating them they sometimes even jumped out of his mouth.

At this sight Pinocchio was filled with such great and unexpected joy that he became almost delirious. He wanted to laugh, he wanted to cry, he wanted to say a thousand things, and instead he could only stammer out a few confused and broken words. At last he succeeded in uttering a cry of joy, and opening his arms he threw them round the little old man's neck and began to shout:

'Oh, my dear papa! I have found you at last! I will never leave you more, nevermore, nevermore!'

'Then my eyes tell me true?' said the little old man, rubbing his eyes; 'then you are really my dear Pinocchio?'

'Yes, yes, I am Pinocchio, really Pinocchio! And you have

'Oh, my dear papa!   I have found you at last!'

quite forgiven me, haven't you? Oh, my dear papa, how good
you are! . . . and to think that I, on the contrary . . . Oh! but if
you only knew what misfortunes have been poured on my head,
and all that has befallen me! Only imagine, the day that you,
poor dear papa, sold your coat to buy me a spelling-book that I
might go to school, I escaped to see the puppet-show, and the
showman wanted to put me on the fire that I might roast his
mutton, and he was the same that afterwards gave me five gold
pieces to take to you, but I met the Fox and the Cat, who took
me to the inn of the Red Crayfish, where they ate like wolves,
and I left by myself in the middle of the night, and I encountered
assassins who ran after me, and I ran away, and they followed,
and I ran, and they always followed me, and I ran, until they
hanged me to a branch of a Big Oak, and the beautiful Little Girl
with blue hair sent a little carriage to fetch me, and the doctors
when they had seen me said immediately, "If he is not dead it is a
proof that he is still alive"—and then by chance I told a lie, and
my nose began to grow until I could no longer get through the
door of the room, for which reason I went with the Fox and the
Cat to bury the four gold pieces, for one I had spent at the inn,
and the Parrot began to laugh, and instead of two thousand gold
pieces I found none left, for which reason the judge when he
heard that I had been robbed had me immediately put in prison
to content the robbers, and then when I was coming away I saw
a beautiful bunch of grapes in a field, and was caught in a trap,

and the peasant, who was quite right, put a dog-collar round my neck that I might guard the poultry-yard, and acknowledging my innocence let me go, and the Serpent with the smoking tail began to laugh and broke a blood-vessel in his chest, and so I returned to the house of the beautiful Little Girl who was dead, and the Pigeon, seeing that I was crying, said to me: "I have seen your father who was building a little boat to go in search of you," and I said to him: "Oh! if I had also wings," and he said to me: "Do you want to go to your father?" and I said: "Without doubt! but who will take me to him?" and he said to me: "I will take you," and I said to him: "How?" and he said to me: "Get on my back," and so we flew all night, and then in the morning all the fishermen who were looking out to sea said to me: "There is a poor man in a boat who is on the point of being drowned," and I recognized you at once, even at that distance, for my heart told me, and I made signs to you to return to land—'

'I also recognized you,' said Geppetto, 'and I would willingly have returned to the shore: but what was I to do! The sea was tremendous, and a great wave upset my boat. Then a horrible Shark who was near, as soon as he saw me in the water, came towards me, and putting out his tongue took hold of me, and swallowed me as if I had been a meat pasty.'

'And how long have you been shut up here?' asked Pinocchio.

'Since that day—it must be nearly two years ago: two years, my dear Pinocchio, that have seemed to me like two centuries!'

'And how have you managed to live? And where did you get the candle? And the matches to light it? Who gave them to you?'

'Stop, and I will tell you everything. You must know, then, that in the same storm in which my boat was upset a merchant vessel foundered. The sailors were all saved, but the vessel went to the bottom, and the Shark, who had that day an excellent appetite, after he had swallowed me, swallowed also the vessel——'

'How?'

'He swallowed it in one mouthful, and the only thing that he spat out was the mainmast, that had stuck between his teeth like a fish-bone. Fortunately for me the vessel was laden with preserved meat in tins, biscuits, bottles of wine, dried raisins, cheese, coffee, sugar, candles, and boxes of wax matches. With this providential supply I have been able to live for two years. But I have arrived at the end of my resources: there is nothing left in the larder, and this candle that you see burning is the last that re-mains——'

'And after that?'

'After that, dear boy, we shall both remain in the dark.'

'Then, dear little papa,' said Pinocchio, 'there is no time to lose. We must think of escaping——'

'Of escaping? . . . and how?'

'We must escape through the mouth of the Shark, throw ourselves into the sea, and swim away.'

'You talk well: but, dear Pinocchio, I don't know how to swim.'

'What does that matter? . . . I am a good swimmer, and you can get on my shoulders and I will carry you safely to shore.'

'All illusions, my boy!' replied Geppetto, shaking his head, with a melancholy smile. 'Do you suppose it possible that a pup-pet like you, scarcely a yard high, could have the strength to swim with me on his shoulders?'

'Try it and you will see?'

Without another word Pinocchio took the candle in his hand, and going in front to light the way he said to his father:

'Follow me, and don't be afraid.'

And they walked for some time and traversed the body and the stomach of the Shark. But when they had arrived at the point where the monster's big throat began, they thought it better to stop to give a good look round and to choose the best moment for escaping.

Now I must tell you that the Shark, being very old, and suf-fering from asthma and palpitation of the heart, was obliged to sleep with his mouth open. Pinocchio, therefore, having ap-proached the entrance to his throat and looking up, could see be-yond the enormous gaping mouth a large piece of starry sky and beautiful moonlight.

'This is the moment to escape,' he whispered, turning to his father; 'the Shark is sleeping like a dormouse, the sea is calm, and it is as light as day. Follow me, dear papa, and in a short time we shall be in safety.'

They immediately climbed up the throat of the sea-monster,

and having reached his immense mouth they began to walk on tiptoe down his tongue.

Before taking the final leap the puppet said to his father:

'Get on my shoulders and put your arms tight round my neck. I will take care of the rest.'

As soon as Geppetto was firmly settled on his son's shoulders, Pinocchio, feeling sure of himself, threw himself into the water and began to swim. The sea was as smooth as oil, the moon shone brilliantly, and the Shark was sleeping so profoundly that even a cannonade would have failed to wake him.

XXXVI

PINOCCHIO AT LAST CEASES TO BE A PUPPET AND BECOMES A BOY.

WHILST PINOCCHIO was swimming quickly towards the shore he discovered that his father, who was on his shoulders with his legs in the water, was trembling as violently as if the poor man had got an attack of ague fever.

Was he trembling from cold or from fear? . . . Perhaps a little from both the one and the other. But Pinocchio, thinking that it was from fear, said to comfort him:

'Courage, papa! In a few minutes we shall be safely on shore.'

'But where is this blessed shore?' asked the little old man, becoming still more frightened, and screwing up his eyes as tailors do when they wish to thread a needle. 'I have been looking in every direction and I see nothing but the sky and the sea.'

'But I see the shore as well,' said the puppet. 'You must know that I am like a cat: I see better by night than by day.'

Poor Pinocchio was making a pretence of being in good spirits, but in reality . . . in reality he was beginning to feel discouraged: his strength was failing, he was gasping and panting for breath . . . he could do no more, and the shore was still far off.

He swam until he had no breath left; then he turned his head to Geppetto and said in broken words:

'Papa . . . help me . . . I am dying!'

The father and son were on the point of drowning when they heard a voice like a guitar out of tune saying:

'Who is it that is dying?'

'It's me, and my poor father!'

'I know that voice! You are Pinocchio!'

'Precisely: and you?'

'I am the Tunny, your prison companion in the body of the Shark.'

'And how did you manage to escape?'

'I followed your example. You showed me the road, and I escaped after you.'

'Tunny, you have arrived at the right moment! I implore you to help us, or we are lost.'

'Willingly and with all my heart. You must, both of you, take hold of my tail and leave me to guide you. I will take you on shore in four minutes.'

Geppetto and Pinocchio, as I need not tell you, accepted the offer at once; but instead of holding on by his tail they thought it would be more comfortable to get on the Tunny's back.

Having reached the shore Pinocchio sprang first on land that he might help his father to do the same. He then turned to the Tunny, and said to him in a voice full of emotion:

'My friend, you have saved my papa's life. I can find no words with which to thank you properly. Permit me at least to give you a kiss as a sign of my eternal gratitude! . . .'

The Tunny put his head out of the water, and Pinocchio, kneeling on the ground, kissed him tenderly on the mouth. At this spontaneous proof of warm affection, the poor Tunny, who was not accustomed to it, felt extremely touched, and ashamed to let himself be seen crying like a child, he plunged under the water and disappeared.

By this time the day had dawned. Pinocchio then offering his arm to Geppetto, who had scarcely breath to stand, said to him:

'Lean on my arm, dear papa, and let us go. We will walk very slowly like the ants, and when we are tired we can rest by the wayside.'

'And where shall we go?' asked Geppetto.

'In search of some house or cottage, where they will out of charity give us a mouthful of bread, and a little straw to serve as a bed.'

They had not gone a hundred yards when they saw by the roadside two villainous-looking individuals begging.

They were the Cat and the Fox, but they were scarcely recognizable. Fancy! the Cat had so long feigned blindness that she had become blind in reality; and the Fox, old, mangy, and with one side paralysed, had not even his tail left. That sneaking thief, having fallen into the most squalid misery, one fine day had found himself obliged to sell his beautiful tail to a travelling pedlar, who bought it to drive away flies.

'Oh, Pinocchio!' cried the Fox, 'give a little in charity to two poor infirm people.'

'Infirm people,' repeated the Cat.

'Be off with you, impostors!' answered the puppet. 'You took me in once, but you will never catch me again.'

'Believe me, Pinocchio, we are now poor and unfortunate indeed!'

'If you are poor, you deserve it. Recollect the proverb: "Stolen money never bears fruit." Begone, impostors!'

And thus saying Pinocchio and Geppetto went their way in peace. When they had gone another hundred yards they saw, at the end of a path in the middle of the fields, a nice little straw hut with a roof of tiles and bricks.

'That hut must be inhabited by someone,' said Pinocchio. 'Let's go and knock at the door.'

They went and knocked.

'Who's there?' said a little voice from within.

'We are a poor father and son without bread and without a roof,' answered the puppet.

'Turn the key and the door will open,' said the same little voice.

Pinocchio turned the key and the door opened. They went in and looked here, there, and everywhere, but could see no one.

'Oh! where is the master of the house?' said Pinocchio, much surprised.

'Here I am up here!'

The father and son looked immediately up to the ceiling, and there on a beam they saw the Talking Cricket.

'Oh, my dear little Cricket!' said Pinocchio, bowing politely to him.

'Ah! now you call me your dear little Cricket. But do you remember the time when you threw a hammer at me, to drive me from your house?'

'You are right, Cricket! Drive me away also . . . throw a hammer at me; but have pity on my poor papa——'

'I will have pity on both father and son, but I wished to remind you of the ill-treatment I received from you, to teach you that in this world, when it is possible, we should show courtesy to everybody, if we wish it to be extended to us in our hour of need.'

'You are right, Cricket, you are right, and I will bear in mind the lesson you have given me. But tell me how you managed to buy this beautiful hut.'

'This hut was given to me yesterday by a goat whose wool was of a beautiful blue colour.'

'And where has the goat gone?' asked Pinocchio with lively curiosity.

'I do not know.'

'And when will it come back?'

'It will never come back. It went away yesterday in great grief and, bleating, it seemed to say: "Poor Pinocchio . . . I shall never see him more . . . by this time the Shark must have devoured him!"'

'Did it really say that? . . . Then it was she! . . . it was she! . . . it was my dear little Fairy!' exclaimed Pinocchio, crying and sobbing.

When he had cried for some time he dried his eyes, and prepared a comfortable bed of straw for Geppetto to lie down upon. Then he asked the Cricket:

'Tell me, little Cricket, where can I find a tumbler of milk for my poor papa?'

'Three fields off from here there lives a gardener called Giangio who keeps cows. Go to him and you will get the milk you are in need of.'

Pinocchio ran all the way to Giangio's house; and the gardener asked him:

'How much milk do you want?'

'I want a tumblerful.'

'A tumbler of milk costs a halfpenny. Begin by giving me the halfpenny.'

'I have not even a farthing,' replied Pinocchio, grieved and mortified.

'That is bad, puppet,' answered the gardener. 'If you have not even a farthing I have not even a drop of milk.'

'I must have patience!' said Pinocchio, and he turned to go.

'Wait a little,' said Giangio. 'We can come to an arrangement together. Will you undertake to turn the pumping machine?'

'What is the pumping machine?'

'It is a wooden pole which serves to draw up the water from the cistern to water the vegetables.'

'You can try me.'

'Well, then, if you will draw a hundred buckets of water I will give you in return a tumbler of milk.'

'It is a bargain.'

Giangio then led Pinocchio to the kitchen garden and taught him how to turn the pumping machine. Pinocchio immediately began to work; but before he had drawn up the hundred buckets of water the perspiration was pouring from his head to his feet. Never before had he undergone such fatigue.

'Up to now,' said the gardener, 'the labour of turning the pumping machine was performed by my little donkey; but the poor animal is dying.'

'Will you take me to see him?' said Pinocchio.

'Willingly.'

When Pinocchio went into the stable he saw a beautiful little donkey stretched on the straw, worn out from hunger and over-work. After looking at him earnestly he said to himself, much troubled:

'I am sure I know this little donkey! His face is not new to me.'

And bending over him he asked him in donkey language:

'Who are you?'

At this question the little donkey opened his dying eyes, and answered in broken words in the same language:

'I am . . . Can . . . dle . . . wick.'

And having again closed his eyes he expired.

'Oh, poor Candlewick!' said Pinocchio in a low voice; and taking a handful of straw he dried a tear that was rolling down his face.

'Do you grieve for a donkey that cost you nothing?' said the gardener. 'What must it be to me who bought him for ready money?'

'I must tell you . . . he was my friend!'

'Your friend?'

'One of my schoolfellows! . . .'

'How?' shouted Giangio, laughing loudly. 'How? had you donkeys for schoolfellows? . . . I can imagine what wonderful lessons yours must have been.

The puppet, who felt much mortified at these words, did not answer; but taking his tumbler of milk, still quite warm, he returned to the hut.

And from that day for more than five months he continued to get up at daybreak every morning to go and turn the pumping machine, to earn the tumbler of milk that was of such benefit to his father in his bad state of health. Nor was he satisfied with this; for during the time that he had over he learnt to make hampers and baskets of rushes, and with the money he obtained by selling them he was able with great economy to provide for all the daily expenses. Amongst other things he constructed an elegant little wheel-chair, in which he could take his father out on fine days to breathe a mouthful of fresh air.

By his industry, ingenuity, and his anxiety to work and to overcome difficulties, he not only succeeded in maintaining his father, who continued infirm, in comfort, but he also contrived to put aside forty pence to buy himself a new coat.

One morning he said to his father:

'I am going to the neighbouring market to buy myself a jacket, a cap, and a pair of shoes. When I return,' he added, laughing, 'I shall be so well dressed that you will take me for a fine gentleman.'

And leaving the house he began to run merrily and happily along. All at once he heard himself called by name, and turning round he saw a big Snail crawling out from the hedge.

'Don't you know me?' asked the Snail.

'It seems to me . . . and yet I am not sure——'

'Do you not remember the Snail who was lady's-maid to the Fairy with blue hair? Do you not remember the time when I came downstairs to let you in, and you were caught by your foot which you had stuck through the house door?'

'I remember it all,' shouted Pinocchio. 'Tell me quickly, my lovely little Snail, where have you left my good Fairy? What is she doing? has she forgiven me? does she still remember me? does she still wish me well? is she far from here? can I go and see her?'

To all these rapid breathless questions the Snail replied in her usual phlegmatic manner:

'My dear Pinocchio, the poor Fairy is lying in bed at the hospital!'

'At the hospital?'

'It is only too true. Overtaken by a thousand misfortunes she has fallen seriously ill, and she has not even enough to buy herself a mouthful of bread.'

'Is it really so? . . . Oh, what sorrow you have given me! Oh, poor Fairy! poor Fairy! poor Fairy! . . . If I had a million I would run and carry it to her . . . but I have only forty pence . . . here they are: I was going to buy a new coat. Take them, Snail, and carry them at once to my good Fairy.'

'And your new coat?'

'What matters my new coat? I would sell even these rags that I have got on to be able to help her. Go, Snail, and be quick; and in two days return to this place, for I hope I shall then be able to give you some more money. Up to this time I have worked to maintain my papa: from to-day I will work five hours more that I may also maintain my good mamma. Goodbye, Snail, I shall expect you in two days.'

The Snail, contrary to her usual habits, began to run like a lizard in a hot August sun.

That evening Pinocchio, instead of going to bed at ten o'clock, sat up till midnight had struck; and instead of making eight baskets of rushes he made sixteen.

Then he went to bed and fell asleep. And whilst he slept he thought that he saw the Fairy smiling and beautiful, who, after having kissed him, said to him:

'Well done, Pinocchio! To reward you for your good heart I

will forgive you for all that is past. Boys who minister tenderly to their parents, and assist them in their misery and infirmities, are deserving of great praise and affection, even if they cannot be cited as examples of obedience and good behaviour. Try and do better in the future and and you will be happy.'

At this moment his dream ended, and Pinocchio opened his eyes and awoke.

But imagine his astonishment when upon awakening he discovered that he was no longer a wooden puppet, but that he had become instead a boy, like all other boys. He gave a glance round and saw that the straw walls of the hut had disappeared, and that he was in a pretty little room furnished and arranged with a simplicity that was almost elegance. Jumping out of bed he found a new suit of clothes ready for him, a new cap, and a pair of new leather boots that fitted him beautifully.

He was hardly dressed when he naturally put his hands in his pockets, and pulled out a little ivory purse on which these words were written: 'The Fairy with blue hair returns the forty pence to her dear Pinocchio, and thanks him for his good heart.' He opened the purse, and instead of forty copper pennies he saw forty shining gold pieces fresh from the mint.

He then went and looked at himself in the glass, and he thought he was someone else. For he no longer saw the usual reflection of a wooden puppet; he was greeted instead by the image of a bright intelligent boy with chestnut hair, blue eyes, and looking as happy and joyful as if it were the Easter holidays.

In the midst of all these wonders succeeding each other Pinocchio felt quite bewildered, and he could not tell if he was really awake or if he was dreaming with his eyes open.

'Where can my papa be?' he exclaimed suddenly, and going into the next room he found old Geppetto quite well, lively, and in good humour, just as he had been formerly. He had already resumed his trade of wood-carving, and he was designing a rich and beautiful frame of leaves, flowers, and animals' heads.

'Tell me, dear papa,' said Pinocchio, throwing his arms round his neck and covering him with kisses; 'how can this sudden change be accounted for?'

'This sudden change in our home is all your doing,' answered Geppetto.

'How my doing?'

'Because when boys who have behaved badly turn over a new leaf and become good they have the power of bringing content and happiness to their families.'

'And where has the old wooden Pinocchio hidden himself?'

'There he is,' answered Geppetto, and he pointed to a big puppet leaning against a chair, with its head on one side, its arms dangling, and its legs so crossed and bent that it was really a miracle that it remained standing.

Pinocchio turned and looked at it; and after he had looked at it for a short time he said to himself happily:

'How ridiculous I was when I was a puppet! and how glad I am that I have become a nice little boy!'

THE END

FOR THE BEST IN PAPERBACKS, LOOK FOR THE

In every corner of the world, on every subject under the sun, Penguin represents quality and variety—the very best in publishing today.

For complete information about books available from Penguin—including Penguin Classics, Penguin Compass, and Puffins—and how to order them, write to us at the appropriate address below. Please note that for copyright reasons the selection of books varies from country to country.

In the United States: Please write to *Penguin Group (USA), P.O. Box 12289 Dept. B, Newark, New Jersey 07101-5289* or call 1-800-788-6262.

In the United Kingdom: Please write to *Dept. EP, Penguin Books Ltd, Bath Road, Harmondsworth, West Drayton, Middlesex UB7 0DA.*

In Canada: Please write to *Penguin Books Canada Ltd, 10 Alcorn Avenue, Suite 300, Toronto, Ontario M4V 3B2.*

In Australia: Please write to *Penguin Books Australia Ltd, P.O. Box 257, Ringwood, Victoria 3134.*

In New Zealand: Please write to *Penguin Books (NZ) Ltd, Private Bag 102902, North Shore Mail Centre, Auckland 10.*

In India: Please write to *Penguin Books India Pvt Ltd, 11 Panchsheel Shopping Centre, Panchsheel Park, New Delhi 110 017.*

In the Netherlands: Please write to *Penguin Books Netherlands bv, Postbus 3507, NL-1001 AH Amsterdam.*

In Germany: Please write to *Penguin Books Deutschland GmbH, Metzlerstrasse 26, 60594 Frankfurt am Main.*

In Spain: Please write to *Penguin Books S. A., Bravo Murillo 19, 1° B, 28015 Madrid.*

In Italy: Please write to *Penguin Italia s.r.l., Via Benedetto Croce 2, 20094 Corsico, Milano.*

In France: Please write to *Penguin France, Le Carré Wilson, 62 rue Benjamin Baillaud, 31500 Toulouse.*

In Japan: Please write to *Penguin Books Japan Ltd, Kaneko Building, 2-3-25 Koraku, Bunkyo-Ku, Tokyo 112.*

In South Africa: Please write to *Penguin Books South Africa (Pty) Ltd, Private Bag X14, Parkview, 2122 Johannesburg.*